Emma Fraser willingly accompanies her spoilt cousin Anne to Russia in 1761, where she is to marry Prince Nikolai Adashev, for it can hardly be worse than her present life as unpaid drudge.

On their arrival in St Petersburg she is horrified to find that the man she took to be a fellow servant is Prince Michael, head of the House of Adashev. It is Michael who has arranged Anne's marriage, and he has plans for Emma too . . . But how can she trust him when he has already deceived her once? Especially when he seems to be so closely involved with the Czarina Catherine.

As Catherine's struggle for control of the country intensifies Emma is caught up in the fierce battle—and the man she most mistrusts is the one man she finds irresistible.

By the same author in Masquerade:

FRANCESCA
MADELON
GAMBLER'S PRIZE
A PRIDE OF MACDONALDS
THE COUNTESS
MARIA ELENA
CASTLE OF THE MIST
MOONSHADOW

Prince of Deception

Valentina Luellen

MILLS & BOON LIMITED
London · Sydney · Toronto

First published in Great Britain 1982
by Mills & Boon Limited, 15–16 Brook's Mews,
London W1A 1DR

ISBN 0 263 73805 1

Set in 10 on 10½ pt Times

Photoset by Rowland Phototypesetting Ltd
Bury St Edmunds, Suffolk.
Made and Printed in Great Britain by
Cox & Wyman Ltd, Reading

CHAPTER ONE

THE man who stepped through the doorway of the inn as Emma came downstairs was so tall it was necessary for him to duck his head beneath the wooden beams surmounting the entrance. He stood, hands on his hips, in the dimly lighted room, surveying the only other occupants—two poorly-dressed serfs huddled at a corner table eating watery soup and black bread and oblivious to the new arrival.

His long fur cloak, covered in snow, swept the dirt floor, and his hat, pulled well down over his features to protect them from the raging storm outside, shadowed his face from her view. After a moment he removed both and tossed them into the arms of the young lad who had followed close on his heels, together with a woman companion, both well shrouded against the unfriendly elements. Beneath his cloak he wore dark hide breeches and a leather jacket and knee-length black boots.

He had the bearing of a soldier, she thought, or a nobleman. The landlord came running to meet him, bowing profusely. The inn-keeper had kept Emma waiting when she arrived and when he had eventually shown himself, his manner had been surly and unhelpful. He had no knowledge of English and his French was so atrocious she could only understand one word out of ten. How different was the reception for this newcomer.

Her curious gaze remained rivetted on the stranger. She moved back into the shadows as he stepped towards the enormous iron stove at the far end of the room. As the light from an overhanging lamp illuminated him clearly for the first time, she saw his hair, thick and dark, the deeply tanned face strong and sensuous. The eyes which suddenly swept upwards to where she stood were bright blue, and disturbing in their intensity. Startled, she realised he had been aware of her ever since the moment he entered.

His attention remained centred on her as he spoke to the inn-keeper. Emma could not follow the exchange of Russian which followed. She was finding the language as difficult to understand as the dour-faced people she had so far encountered.

Many times over the past four months she had wondered why she had not left the Tarrant household the moment she was told of the preposterous suggestion that she should leave England and make her home in Russia. Then she had looked into the pale, unhappy face of her cousin and known, despite the humiliation poured down on the head of a poor relation—which is what she was—the years of servitude, of being little more than an unpaid servant in the house of her own aunt and uncle, she could not abandon the helpless girl to the rigours of the exhausting, often frightening journey across Europe to her new homeland, and the Russian nobleman she was to marry.

It was November 1761 and the countryside was experiencing one of the harshest winters ever known. Snow and ice covered the roads, making travelling not only dangerous but at times impossible. The port of Kronstadt was completely ice-bound, stranding the Russian fleet in harbour, and making it inaccessible to other shipping, which is why they had been forced to take the drastic action of proceeding overland to St Petersburg in a draughty, uncomfortable coach. Had she not been a sensibly-minded woman, Emma might have wondered at the train of events which had made the journey so nerve-racking.

First, there had been a heavy fall of snow which completely blocked the road ahead and had taken a whole day to clear. Then there came the sudden illness of the only other passenger, an old man who had coughed and sneezed from morning to night. He had been left behind at a farmhouse when it became clear he was in no condition to travel further. The final irritation, which stretched patience and frayed tempers to the limit, was the collapse of the axle when the coach was only twenty-five miles from St Petersburg. Luckily they had been in sight of a village when the accident occurred. The driver led Emma and her cousin through knee-deep snow to the sanctuary of the local inn and there left them to fend for themselves while he went off to find a blacksmith.

Emma had immediately asked for the best room, overcoming her disappointment at the cold, unfriendly reception which greeted them, and her apprehension as she studied their surroundings. The place was filthy, the floor strewn with dirty straw, and there was an unpleasant aroma of strong ale.

Her cousin threw a fit of hysteria when they were shown into the 'best room', and it took Emma almost half-an-hour to calm her. The room was as disgusting as those below. The drapes around the fourposter bed were full of dust, and Emma suspected the blankets had not been washed for months. Smoke belched from an antiquated stove, and she found the window was too stiff to open to admit fresh air.

She had asked for food to be brought to them, but the landlord had gone away without a word and as time passed she realised he had either not understood or had deliberately ignored the request; which was why she had ventured downstairs again. Had it not been for the fact that neither of them had eaten since that morning, nothing would have induced her to leave the bedroom, despite its sordidness, until morning came and they were able to continue on their way in the repaired coach.

'You look lost, mademoiselle.' From the chair he had pulled up before the stove, his long legs stretched out towards the warmth of the fire, the stranger looked up at her once again.

'Oh, thank goodness—you speak French,' Emma exclaimed. She was so delighted to hear a friendly voice she completely ignored the folly of her action in speaking to him.

He looked respectable enough, but she had been warned the countryside was full of robbers and starving peasants who would slit the throats of unsuspecting travellers for the clothes on their backs.

'I am quite harmless.' A smile tugged at the corners of the lean mouth as she hesitated on the stairs. 'Come down and warm yourself. You look frozen.'

'Our stove is being tiresome, it is filling the whole room with smoke. I was hoping the landlord could do something about it . . . and he seems to have forgotten about our food . . .'

Slowly she approached him. She was cold despite the thick, woollen cloak she was hugging about her body. The man stood up, motioning she should take his seat. Close to, she realised he was over six feet. She barely came up to his shoulder and felt dwarfed.

'No—I cannot stay,' she said quickly. 'I must go back upstairs to my cousin . . .' Anne would throw another tantrum if she was absent for long!

'Where are your servants? Asleep outside? Jan, go and wake the lazy scoundrels,' he ordered, turning to the youth who had come in with him.

'No. You do not understand,' Emma protested. 'We have no servants.'

'Two women—travelling alone in this part of the country—in weather not fit for dogs! Are you both mad?' The bronzed features registered incredulity.

Had she not been so tired and hungry, Emma would have taken offence at the remark. It was not her fault the manservant the Tarrants had sent with them had refused to leave the ship when it docked, declaring his intention to return to civilisation at the first opportunity. Or that the escort which should have been there to meet them had not arrived after two whole days of tedious waiting. Emma had been driven to distraction by her cousin's constant complaining. She had endured tears and threats and endless moods, until at last she agreed they should continue to St Petersburg by themselves. She had been provided with sufficient funds for the journey and was confident of her own ability to look after them both. It was no more than she had been doing since they were children. Her confidence and her patience had both been stretched to their limits by the time they reached the inn.

'Not mad, I assure you, sir,' she replied with quiet dignity. 'My cousin and I are on our way to St Petersburg, but because the port at Kronstadt is frozen we are forced to travel by road. The choice was not ours, and we should have been met . . .' she broke off as the man before her gave a surprised oath.

'Devil take me for a fool! Are you both English?'

'Why—yes. My cousin is Miss Anne Tarrant. She is going to St Petersburg to marry Prince Nikolai Adashev.'

Before she could determine his intentions, he had reached out and pushed back the hood covering her head. Freed from confinement, waist-length hair as black and gleaming as a raven's wing tumbled past Emma's shoulders. Its darkness accentuated the pallor of her cheeks, the shadows beneath her eyes, which betrayed the exhaustion she stubbornly refused to acknowledge.

'Forgive me. I did not recognise you.'

'Recognise me?' Emma echoed. 'We have never met before, sir.'

'No, that is true, but I was given descriptions of the two women I was to meet.' The stranger drew himself up and gave a slight bow. 'I have come to take you to Prince Adashev.'

Emma's eyes darted to the boy and his woman companion. The latter had unfastened her cloak and pushed aside the hood. She wore a brightly patterned skirt and a white blouse. Her face was similar to many Emma had seen from the window of the coach: slightly slanted eyes, high cheekbones and a full, wide mouth. Of Circassian or Mongolian extraction, she suspected. The youth was what she had expected a Russian to look like: dark hair and eyes, stoic-faced and inclined to sullenness.

'Well,' the dark-haired man before her gave a frown of annoyance. 'Did you not hear me, girl? I am to escort you safely to St Petersburg. If you had both been less foolhardy and remained on the coast, you would not now find yourself in this pig-sty.'

'You were late. I did not know what to do,' Emma protested, in defence of her actions.

'So it's you I have to thank for the fact I have been chasing all over the countryside trying to intercept your coach. Never mind, it's done now. You are Mademoiselle Fraser, are you not?'

'Emma Fraser. And you, sir?'

'You may call me Michael. I have gifts for your mistress from the Prince. And food and fresh coffee outside in the troikas. Be good enough to tell her I have arrived and will see her while Jan unpacks. Unless, of course, you prefer to sample the hog-swill you will be served here,' he added, as Emma did not move.

He was no gentleman, but a servant like herself, and yet he was acting the Grand-Seigneur! It annoyed her.

'Miss Tarrant was resting when I left her. I will tell her you have arrived at last. Please present yourself in ten minutes.'

She saw his mouth tighten at her polite, but icy tone. For a moment those piercing blue eyes held hers, challenging her authority to speak to him in such a tone. He was not to know, had fate not decreed otherwise, the roles would have been reversed. Anne, the servant, and Emma on her way to marry a Prince descended from the Royal House of Rurik. There were times when the past rose up to taunt and rouse the devil in her. She held her ground, grey eyes smouldering with resentment, head thrown back, defiance blazing out of her young face, but the spirited moment died as quickly as it had been brought to life. Gathering her cloak about her she brushed past him and ran upstairs. She did not look back, yet she knew his eyes still followed her. She could feel them.

Her cousin was still huddled in the only chair the room possessed, exactly as when Emma had left her. The cases remained unopened, and the stove continued to pour choking smoke into the room. She flung wide the door in an effort to clear it and went down on one knee before Anne Tarrant. There was scarcely a year between them, yet there were times when Emma felt twice her nineteen years.

Lord and Lady Tarrant had spoiled their only daughter from the moment she came into the world, red-faced and howling lustily. She had wanted for nothing. Clothes, toys, governesses, the best tutors who had tried—and failed more often than not—to instil in her some appreciation of the arts and languages. She was doted on by an adoring father, spoiled by an over-indulgent mother. Emma grew up in her shadow. By the time she was ten she had learned to accept that she would always be poor and probably have to earn a living for the rest of her life.

The Tarrants were good to her once she no longer repudiated their condemnation of her mother and the disgraceful marriage she had contracted, of which Emma was the result. In return for food and a roof over her head, she did whatever was required of her. The resentment she had once harboured at their treatment of her had died long ago. Even Anne's spiteful comments when she thought Emma was rising above her station failed to arouse any response. She kept her thoughts, her dreams, her heartaches, to herself. Each new day which dawned she treated as an adventure, a challenge. While Anne yawned and complained to her tutors, Emma sat in the background, listened intently and learned, often studying French and Latin into the early hours upstairs in her small attic room.

Her needlework was praised by all who saw it, and on more than one occasion a dress she had made for her cousin was so well received, she was called upon to make another. Emma Fraser, beloved daughter of a titled lady and a Scottish soldier, reduced to the menial work of a seamstress! There were times when Emma wanted to rip the lovely clothes she made to pieces, tear into shreds the exquisite lace it gave her so much pleasure to create.

Anne Tarrant had cried herself into a state of lethargy. She obstinately refused Emma's attempts to remove her cloak. She was pale and dull-eyed. Her lovely red hair had not been dressed properly for several days and her blue travelling dress was creased from the many hours spent in the coach.

'You must let me make you look presentable,' Emma insisted, quashing the urge to shake some life into her. If she was not complaining or finding fault with everything Emma did and said, she withdrew into a moody silence. She had not wanted to marry a Russian Prince, no matter how noble his birthright, nor leave the comfort of her home in England and everything she had ever known to begin a new life in a strange country.

Throughout the journey she had refused to accept the fact she would never see England again, and surrounded herself with memories of the past instead of thoughts of the future. Emma pulled off her cloak and threw it across the bed. Delving into one of the valises she found Anne's silver-backed brush and mirror and an ivory comb.

'Let me brush your hair. Whatever will he think of you in this state?'

'Who? Leave me alone. I am hungry. I want to eat and then go to bed,' her cousin returned ungraciously.

'Be still.' Emma loosened the fiery tresses from the tortoiseshell combs holding them in place and began to brush out the tangles. 'Prince Nikolai has sent someone to meet us. He is downstairs now. There, doesn't that feel better?'

'So, my future husband has deigned to supply an escort after all. Well, you can tell his messenger I am too tired to receive him. Let him wait as I have had to.'

'You cannot do that,' Emma protested, aghast. 'He

has come a long way and he wasn't too pleased he had to waste time looking for us. I told him he could come up in ten minutes. He has gifts from the Prince . . . and some decent food.'

Emma did not know if it was the thought of the gifts or the food which attracted Anne more, but she was allowed to finish her cousin's toilette in peace and quiet.

'You may tell the Prince's errand-boy I will see him now,' Anne declared, taking a final look at her appearance in the mirror Emma held.

She was taller than the other girl, with a willowy grace which had turned many a head. A year spent with relatives in France, when she had been introduced at court, had first awakened in her the knowledge of her own beauty—and how to use it. When it suited her she could be gay and amusing, but her manner could change in an instant, revealing not far beneath the surface a vindictive child who revelled in causing pain to those poor unfortunates who fell from favour. Emma was used to the insults, the contemptuous remarks which often referred to the disgrace her mother had brought to the family. She bore them in silence, praying for the day she would be free to make a life of her own.

She put down the mirror, and then something made her look towards the open door. The stranger stood there, silently surveying them both. Behind him were the woman and the boy, Jan, who held a large wicker basket.

Without waiting to be invited in, the man moved forward to Anne's chair. Emma caught her breath as she saw the flash of annoyance which crossed the haughty features. Even Lord Tarrant had found it necessary to reprimand his daughter concerning her treatment of the servants.

'This is Michael, the messenger from Prince Nikolai,' she said quickly, hoping to avert an unpleasant scene.

'I hope the rest of the Prince's servants have better manners.' Anne's tone was contemptuous. 'You will not come into my presence again without my permission. You are late. Why?'

'That was our fault . . .' Emma began. The look directed her way warned her not to continue.

'It is regrettable you did not remain another day before continuing your journey, Mademoiselle Tarrant. You would have been spared that miserable coach and this . . .' The man called Michael motioned to the shabby room. 'Please accept my apologies for such a poor introduction to my country, and allow me to make amends.'

Emma's eyes widened. He was speaking in English! Faultless English with only the faintest trace of an accent. How much of their conversation had he overheard, she wondered? His expression gave nothing away. From beneath his arm he took a small, brass-hinged casket and flipped back the lid, bending forward so that Anne could clearly see the contents.

'Prince Nikolai hopes you will accept these trinkets as a token of his affection. He is counting the days until you are together.'

Trinkets! Emma thought in astonishment. They looked priceless. She saw rubies and pearls, diamonds set in silver and gold. Anne's eyes widened also. Against them her own pieces of jewellery were mere baubles. Her long, tapered fingers touched a huge diamond pendant.

'It's beautiful,' Emma breathed. 'Oh, do let me put it on for you.'

Her outstretched hand was ignored. Anne bestowed a warm smile on the man before her and held the pendant out to him. A sure sign he had been forgiven his bad manners and his lateness, Emma thought. His smooth tongue and pretty compliments had won her over—not to mention the array of precious stones, glittering and shimmering in the candlelight.

Without a word Michael fastened the jewel around Anne's throat.

'You have chosen well. This piece once belonged to

the Princess Sophia, Prince Nikolai's grandmother. He was sure it would meet with your approval,' he said, stepping back.

Anne gave a slight nod as she caressed the cold stone. She was being treated like royalty and was enjoying every minute of it. The frustrations of the journey slipped away as she took the casket and stared at the contents, considering for the first time since setting foot on Russian soil the advantages of her new position.

'With your permission,' Michael murmured. He beckoned forward the boy. 'I realise your journey will have greatly fatigued you, but you must eat before you rest. Prepare the table, Jan, and then see to that stove. Irene, come and meet your new mistress.'

The woman approached and curtsied low in front of Anne's chair. She took the proffered hand and kissed it reverently, and remained on one knee until Anne indicated she should rise.

'Her name is Irene. She has a little knowledge of English which is why the Prince has sent her to you. She is honest and will serve you faithfully. Her family have been with the Adashev's for many years.'

'I already have a maid, although I must admit there are times when one is barely sufficient for my needs,' Anne returned, not looking at Emma. She hesitated for a moment only. 'Very well, the woman may stay. Emma has yet to finish my trousseau, so I shall need her services.'

Already she was growing dispensable, Emma thought, two fierce spots of colour beginning to burn in her pale cheeks. Quickly she turned away and began to strip the blankets from the bed. They would have to be shaken well before her cousin would condescend to lie on them.

'Leave that,' Michael instructed. 'Irene will see to it later.'

She drew back, resenting his interruption. Was she to take orders from him too?

A ricketty wooden table from beneath the window

was drawn into the centre of the room and covered with a snow-white linen cloth. Emma stood speechless, aware of her cousin's growing astonishment too, as it was laid with an array of food which made her mouth water. Caviar, pickled herrings, pheasant cooked in wine, and cold chicken, all arranged on silver platters. Red wine was poured into exquisitely carved silver goblets and placed beside the eating utensils which, Emma saw, bore a crest on each and every one.

She saw two places had been laid, stood back hesitantly as Michael pulled over a stool and Jan appeared with a sturdy chair, obviously from another room, and stood waiting for them to seat themselves. Not until Anne had done so did she realise she was not intended to eat alone. She looked first at her cousin and then at the silent man at her side and her eyes glittered maliciously.

'You take too much upon yourself. In England servants do not sit at the same table as their betters. Is it different in Russia?'

'No, Mademoiselle Tarrant, in Russia everyone knows their place,' Michael returned. His tone was polite, but Emma saw the blue eyes narrow to angry pinpoints. 'I was under the impression, from the Prince naturally, that Mademoiselle Fraser was not to be treated as such. She is related to you, is she not? Despite the fact she acts as your companion.'

Anne tasted her wine. Her eyes swept Emma from head to toe. With Irene on hand to pander her every whim, she would not be needed once the trousseau was complete, Emma thought—not until another bout of home-sickness sent her rushing to the only friend she had in the world. She was conscious of everyone's eyes on her. Those of Irene, slanted and inscrutable. Jan's, totally disinterested as he turned away to attend to the stove. Anne's, dark with resentment at the fact her unimportant cousin had aroused such attention, and Michael's, still glittering with an anger she did not understand. She could stand the humiliation no longer.

'I will eat downstairs. The landlord has probably prepared some food by now. When you are ready to retire, perhaps you will send Irene to fetch me. If I am required, that is.'

She had the satisfaction of seeing her cousin blush at the taunt as she walked to the door.

She was sitting in front of the stove when Michael came down some while later. No-one had come near her. The two men who had been eating earlier had fallen asleep at their table and the landlord was nowhere to be seen. She felt too miserable to bother to call for him. Jan followed close on the heels of his master and went outside. The opening of the door, brief though it was, sent a blast of chilling air into the room. Emma shivered and bent closer to the fire. He was back in a moment, carrying a smaller basket which he set down on a table beside her. She watched in silence as he brought out two leather-covered wine bottles, crystal glasses and more food. Michael hooked a booted foot behind a chair and dragged it across to him.

'Is my company acceptable, mademoiselle, or would you prefer to eat alone?'

She could only stare at him, lost for words. With a smile he poured out wine for them both and offered her one of the glasses. She took it, but did not touch the contents.

'See the horses are well fed, Jan, we have a hard journey ahead of us tomorrow. And make sure that lazy swine, Igor, stays awake or we may not have any with which to continue our journey.'

The boy nodded and left them. Emma realised she had not heard him utter a single word since he entered the inn.

'He has no tongue,' Michael said, answering her unspoken question. 'His last master cut it out because he was insolent. I found him starving in Moscow six years ago and he has been with me ever since. He is a Cossack from the Ural Mountains—utterly devoted to me, thank God. If he wasn't, I would probably have had a knife in my back before now.'

Emma cautiously sipped her wine. It was sweet and very strong and she could feel it bring immediate warmth to her bones. Was there more to this man than met the eye? Had he been born on the wrong side of the blanket? A love child? Rejected by an aristocratic mother or father? He had the grand manners for it to have happened that way. Had she herself not been told often enough that she did not act the servant, either in her manner or in her thoughts. How could she, when it was so impossible to accept she had no money of her own, no position in life, no title—to forget her mother who once had them all and had given them up for love of a man. Emma had decided long ago she would never permit herself to fall in love.

'I have been with the Prince and his family for many years. I look after the estates mainly. A manager, I suppose you would call me. In Russia such a position of trust is rewarded with little—advantages.'

Michael sliced some cold chicken with a wicked-looking knife taken from his belt, and put several large pieces onto a platter together with a thick wedge of cheese and black bread. He filled another for himself, drained his glass and refilled it.

'Eat, girl,' he ordered. 'You will need all the strength you can get to deal with that shrew upstairs.'

Emma was feeling quite faint from the intense cold and lack of food. Under his watchful gaze she began to eat what he had provided. The chicken, so tender it melted in her mouth, was consumed with relish. The moment her glass was empty it was refilled and she did not object. If she was going to be treated like this in Russia, then she was infinitely better off.

Emma knew little of the contract which had suddenly been sprung upon her cousin, only that she had been seen at the French court by Prince Nikolai's elder brother, who had been so taken with her he had made immediate enquiries as to her identity. By the time they returned to London, he had already visited the Tarrants, asked for her hand on behalf of his brother, and been accepted. Emma had often wondered what had prompted them to accept such an offer. She knew they were almost penniless and had no money for the dowry without which Anne could never marry into the London society with whom she mixed. Perhaps the marriage settlement had been to their advantage? Anne, to her knowledge, had her eye on four or five suitable young men, all wealthy in their own right, two with titles. She did not understand her parents' decision to marry her off to some Russian prince. She had wheedled, cajoled, thrown tantrums, in an effort to make them change their minds. All in vain.

Preparations for her departure had gone ahead, and Emma had been told she was to accompany her. Lord and Lady Tarrant were not to journey with their daughter, nor would they be present at the wedding. Emma thought her cousin would throw a fit when she heard the news. The reason given was Lady Tarrant's failing health which would not stand up to the harshness of the Russian winter. Emma suspected it was lack of money which kept them at home, but she remained silent on the subject.

Michael leaned forward to refill her glass, but she quickly moved it out of his reach.

'I think I have had enough, thank you. I feel quite sleepy. I should go to bed.'

Bed! Where was she to sleep? If Anne would not allow her to sit at the same table, she certainly would not allow her to share the same bed, regardless of the fact they had been forced to do that for most of the journey.

Her companion rose to his feet, stretching his arms above his head with a long sigh. She saw the ripple of muscles beneath the leather jacket. Strong, agile, and attractive . . . Anne would find such a man a challenge.

'How long will it take us to reach St Petersburg?' she asked, reluctantly moving away from the warmth of the fire. Michael retrieved her cloak from the chair and draped it around her shoulders. His fingers accidentally brushed her cheek as he stepped back. She hoped he would think it was the fire or the wine, or a combination of both, that brought a flush of colour to her cheeks.

'A day or two in this weather, although the roads begin to improve from here to the city. Unlike your cousin, I think you are anxious to see your new home.'

'My home,' she echoed softly. 'Yes, I suppose that's what it is. I haven't really had much time to think about it.'

'How easily you have accepted having your life changed overnight, my little English miss,' Michael drawled, and the mockery in his tone stung her. 'Have you no regrets? Nothing you have left behind which was important to you? No young man who will miss those sad eyes?'

'Like you, I am a servant. I go where I am told,' she returned. He had spoiled an enjoyable evening with his stupid remarks.

She hurried upstairs with him close behind. Ignoring her hostile glare, he opened the door of Anne's room and stood back for her to enter. Inside it was very warm. Fresh wood had been piled beside the stove, enough to last all night, she noticed. Remnants of food still lingered on the table, but not very much. Her cousin too, had eaten well. Irene, who had been dozing at the foot of the bed, scrambled to her feet as they entered. Beyond her, wrapped in furs on a clean blanket, Anne slept soundly. A finger against his lips, Michael motioned the woman to go back to sleep. Emma's hand was taken in a firm grip. She tried to free herself, but he gave her an impatient tug and she followed him out of the room.

He led her across the corridor and into a small room which housed a narrow bed against one wall and a chair beneath the tiny window. Releasing her he lighted the candle and then stepped back to the door.

'This is the only other room there is,' he said, matter-of-factly. 'You will be more comfortable here than on the floor back there.'

'But—but this is your room,' Emma exclaimed as she caught sight of his fur hat and cloak thrown across the bed. 'It is very kind of you, but I cannot . . .'

'You can, and you will. I shall sleep downstairs. It is warm and I have another excellent bottle of wine to keep me company. Goodnight, mademoiselle.'

She had no chance to protest further. The door closed behind him and she was alone. Not wanting to take the risk of being bitten to death by whatever infested the bedclothes, she threw them onto the floor, wrapped herself firmly in her cloak and lay down. The mattress was hard, but she was too tired to care. There was no stove in the room. Her finger touched the rich fur cloak belonging to Michael. It was lined throughout and very heavy. She drew it up over her shoulders and within minutes was asleep.

CHAPTER TWO

THE next day the journey continued, not in the draughty, bone-shaking coach, but in a covered sleigh, piled high with bearskin rugs to keep out the cold. There were two troikas, as Emma discovered they were called, drawn by high-stepping horses, whose leather harnesses were adorned with tiny silver bells. Irene and Jan travelled in the first together with the luggage, Anne, Emma and Michael in the second. It was a surprisingly warm and comfortable way to travel, Emma discovered, although her cousin found fault with the fact that the pace was tediously slow. Emma thought the horses made marvellous progress through sleet and snow which made the roads barely negotiable, but she dared not say so. She rarely spoke at all that day to anyone, and her companions also seemed to prefer their own council.

They rested overnight at an inn outside St Petersburg. They were received with smiles and a large open fire to revive flagging spirits and after an enormous meal of a soup called Borsch, containing white cabbage and beetroot, followed by beef, roasted over a spit before their very eyes, they were shown to separate rooms, containing a clean bed and a stove. That night Emma found sleep evaded her. She was too excited. Tomorrow they would be in St Petersburg.

The city lay at the mouth of the River Neva, divided in two by the wide expanse of water which flowed through the centre of it, and was, at this time of the year, completely frozen over. The houses were mostly built of wood, sloping back from the river banks. Emma remembered reading somewhere of the terrible fires which from time to time devastated the city until the Czarina Elizabeth instigated improvements on a grand scale. On the horizon she could just see a spiral of smoke. She shivered and quickly switched her gaze to the houses situated on the tiny islands in the river. A network of bridges criss-crossed to each one, giving easy access to either bank. She could imagine those houses at the height of summer with the gardens full of flowers, swans gliding at the water's edge, boats . . .

'Emma, are you pretending to be deaf on purpose?' Anne demanded irritably.

'I—I am sorry. What did you say? I was daydreaming.' Emma caught sight of Michael's eyes on her and ignored the laughter in them. He had not heard a caustic word from her cousin since they had continued their journey. She wondered if that would have been the case had he been grey haired and sixty?

'Michael says we are almost at the house. Do I look all right? Oh, I knew I should have worn my black—it is so much more sophisticated, but you insisted this green monstrosity was more suitable.'

'The green is very becoming if I may say so,' Michael murmured. 'However, I can inform the Prince of your wish to rest for a while and to change into something more befitting a bride, if you wish. He will understand.'

'Yes, do that. I cannot possibly allow him to see me like this. I shall wear my black, Emma, and my new diamond pendant. Irene can dress my hair while you press the dress.' Anne leaned forward in her seat, eager for her first sight of the Adashev house.

It was a huge, sprawling place, with its own grounds and surrounded by a high wall, set in the shadow of an enormous building which Michael told them was the Winter Palace. In the distance towered the grim, grey-stoned fortress of St Peter and St Paul. No sooner had the troika come to a halt than a liveried footman came running out to meet them. Two young grooms held the prancing horses steady while the two girls alighted, and then led them away.

Michael conducted them up a long flight of stairs, through heavy oak doors into an entrance hall, panelled with mirrors. Above Emma's head the light from hundreds of candles fell from a crystal chandelier. The exterior of the house had been sombre, uninteresting—the inside was luxurious beyond her wildest expectations. Ever since she had seen the jewel casket sent by Prince Nikolai, she had known him to be a man of considerable wealth. But these surroundings went far beyond anything she had ever seen before.

A magnificent marble staircase swept upwards to the floors above. The furniture was mainly of ebony or oak, most pieces intricately carved, and the crest of the Adashev family—a stag's head surmounted by a circlet of leaves—was not only on the furniture and doors, but worn by each of the servants who approached them, to take Anne's cloak and gloves, to carry in the luggage; by the manservant who bowed before them and held out a silver tray bearing a glass of sparkling wine.

'With the compliments of the Prince,' Michael said smilingly. 'Welcome to St Petersburg, Mademoiselle Tarrant. If you will go with Dmitri, he will show you to your rooms. Those of Mademoiselle Fraser you will find adjoin them—for convenience,' he added as annoyance registered on Anne's face.

She was making it clear to Emma she no longer considered her to be of much use.

As they mounted the staircase, Emma glanced at herself in one of the gilt-framed mirrors which lined the walls. She looked a pale and insignificant shadow as she followed the tall, elegant figure of her cousin. She was tired, and it showed in her face, but she knew there would be no rest for her until she had finished the all-important trousseau. The wedding was to be in four weeks time. She would be sewing all the hours God put into a day in order to finish everything before the special day arrived.

They were shown into a suite of rooms, decorated in the style of Louis XIV, the 'Sun King', and reminding

Emma very much of the interior of the palace at Versailles. Anne inspected every room. She scrutinised the huge canopied bed with its silken drapes, the dressing table already arrayed with vases of fresh flowers and tiny glass pots filled with exotic perfumes, and Emma saw her smile to herself. She was well pleased with her reception. First the jewels, now these little tokens from the Prince.

The sitting-room was enormous, tastefully decorated in pale grey and gold. Emma guessed she was thinking of the times when she would entertain her new Russian friends here, dressed in the finest silks and lace, shimmering with jewels—the centre of attraction.

'This will do very nicely.' She threw herself down onto one of the brocade-covered couches and stared at her Russian maid. 'Well, what are you waiting for? I want to get out of these filthy clothes and have my hair brushed. Emma, go and press my black dress at once.'

The silent footman hovering by the door showed Emma through a communicating door into the bedroom. She took off her cloak and began to unpack the dozen or more trunks and valises, of which only one was hers, until she found the gown Anne required for her first meeting with Prince Nikolai Adashev. It was black velvet, beautifully cut, the bodice encrusted with tiny seed pearls. It was severe in its simplicity and not the colour Emma would have chosen to wear as a prospective bride, but it showed off to perfection her cousin's slender shoulders and full breasts—and she knew this.

It was an hour before Emma returned, carrying the dress carefully to the stool where Anne sat while Irene brushed her red hair. She stood in silence, watching as the woman arranged the gleaming tresses in curls and secured them with pearl combs.

The black velvet gave Anne an elegance and grace far beyond her twenty years. She moved slowly around before the cheval mirror, her eyes searching for the slightest wisp of hair out of place, the tiniest crease in the material. Unable to find any fault, she at last moved away.

'You look lovely, Anne,' Emma said sincerely. 'I am sure the Prince will think you more beautiful than the miniature you sent him. How long do you think it will be before he sends for you?'

'Sends for me? I am not one of his household to be summoned at will,' her cousin retorted tight-lipped. 'If he had the manners of a gentleman he would have greeted me when I first arrived, instead of leaving Michael to act in his place. Does he think I intend to remain closeted here until he has the time to meet his future bride? Irene, go and find the Prince, wherever he is, and tell him I am quite refreshed now and wish to see him.'

'Yes, Madame,' the woman answered and left the room. She was gone only a few minutes. 'Prince Nikolai and his brother are waiting for you in the drawing-room, Madame,' she said, upon her return.

'There, you see!' Anne wheeled on Emma triumphantly. 'There are times when you make me sick, do you know that? You are a little mouse—afraid of your own shadow. Go and finish my unpacking.'

'It is the Prince's wish Miss Fraser accompanies you,' Irene said as Anne moved towards the door, and the words brought her to an immediate halt. 'He was most explicit—he wishes to see both English ladies.'

Emma did not hear her cousin's answer as she swept out of the room with a haughty toss of her head. What on earth did Prince Nikolai want with her, she wondered, as she followed at some considerable distance behind? She had no place in his household except as Anne's companion and that position, she suspected, was in jeopardy. Was she about to be told her services were no longer required?

A waiting servant led them to the drawing-room, swung open the massive brass-studded doors and admitted them to the presence of Prince Nikolai Adashev, the future husband of Anne Tarrant.

Emma was pleasantly surprised at her first glimpse of him. Quite tall and broad shouldered, with fair hair and brown eyes which registered instant pleasure the moment they encountered Anne. Diamond rings flashed on the hand he extended towards her. She smiled graciously, allowed him to take her by the hand and draw her into the centre of the room. They liked each other, Emma thought in relief. She had been dreading this moment. After such a long and arduous journey, if either of them did not suit . . .

'My brother told me you were beautiful, but even his colourful description has not done justice to the ray of sunlight which has suddenly entered my life.' His voice was slightly slurred. An impediment of speech—or had he been drinking prior to their arrival? He touched Anne's fingers to his lips, smiling over her shoulder to where Emma hesitated on the threshold. 'And this must be Emma, your cousin. Come in, child, you are doubly welcome for conveying my bride to me. Michael tells me you looked after her like a mother hen. Forgive me, I am forgetting my manners. You have met my brother, have you not . . .?'

The man who rose from the high-backed chair in front of the fire, unseen by either Emma or Anne until that moment, was taller than Nikolai and very dark. The face creased into a smile which mocked their astonishment. The last time Emma had seen him he had been wearing the garb of a servant, now he was dressed in a burgundy coloured velvet jacket and doeskin breeches, and looked every inch a gentleman. The blue eyes ignored Anne. They were centred on Emma's face as he spoke.

'We exchanged first names only, Nikolai. Perhaps I should have presented myself correctly, mesdemoiselles. I am Prince Michael Adashev . . .'

'You!' Anne's voice was no more than a harsh, angry whisper. 'How dare you! I have been grossly insulted.' She spun on Emma, quivering with rage. 'You knew, didn't you? How you must have laughed at me behind my back. Mama always said you were not to be trusted . . .'

'Anne—you don't know what you are saying,' Emma

cried, horrified at the unjust insinuation. 'I would never have deceived you had I known who he really was.' She turned appealingly to Michael, whose face now registered displeasure at the outburst. He was the elder brother who had seen Anne in France! He had arranged the match and no doubt wished to reassure himself the decision had been the correct one by spying on them at the inn. The cruelty of the deliberate deception—for that is what it appeared to be—angered her, not only on Anne's behalf, but also on her own. For a while she had begun to think she might have found a friend in this new land.

'Tell her—she will believe you,' she said.

'What either of you chooses to believe is of little consequence,' came the chilling answer. 'As head of this family, I answer to no-one for my actions.'

Anne tore herself free from Nikolai's grasp and stepped back. He followed, trying to detain her. Emma saw her cousin grow exceedingly pale at his unsteady gait. Not only was he limping heavily, but it was now obvious to them both that he had been drinking for some considerable time. A drunkard and a cripple—the revulsion on Anne's face was there for all to see.

'Why don't you show Anne your wedding gift,' Michael suggested. His hand rested reassuringly for a moment on his brother's shoulder. Nikolai gave a nod and once again stretched out a hand towards Anne. It was ignored.

'There will be no wedding,' she said in a flat tone. 'Emma, go upstairs and begin repacking. We are leaving immediately.'

'And where will you go?' Michael enquired coolly, unperturbed by the announcement. 'You have been brought here to marry my brother, and marry him you will. Put all thoughts of going back to England out of your mind once and for all. This is your home now. I suggest you accept it with good grace.'

Nikolai Adashev turned away from them and walked unsteadily to the long, oak sideboard against the far wall. The polished surface held several pieces of silver plate, glass decanters and silver-crested goblets. He seized one of the latter, filled it to the brim with wine and drank deeply. His eyes were cold and hard as he stared across the room at his future bride, no sign of friendliness now. Slowly he considered her, from the top of her shining red hair to the hem of her black gown. By the time his inspection had finished Anne's cheeks were flaming with embarrassment. No man had ever subjected her to such detailed scrutiny before—at least not face to face.

'You are right,' he said filling his goblet again. 'She does have good hips. She should breed well.'

Breed! As if she was an animal. The insult was intended to hurt and it did. Anne swayed back and only Emma's arms prevented her from falling. Bright tears rushed to her eyes. She fought for words, could find none to express the disgust she felt at her position, and burst into tears instead.

'I will not stay . . . I will not.' Wrenching herself from Emma's arms, she ran to the door, pulled it open and almost knocked over the startled servant waiting outside.

'A shrew . . . and a spoilt one at that. My poor Nikolai, what have I given you for a wife?' Michael drawled humourlessly. 'You had better go after her—give her your gift. The sight of a few emeralds will appease her wounded pride if I am any judge of character.'

'You, sir, are not capable of judging her character or anyone else's,' Emma retorted, her voice trembling a little. 'She is a lady, not one of your serfs. Your treatment of her is despicable.'

'You forget to whom you are speaking, girl,' Michael snapped.

'Pray remind me then, sir, for I find it a trifle confusing. At the inn you presented yourself as one of Prince Nikolai's servants—the manager of the Adashev estates, is that not what you called yourself? Not once did you give any indication of the closer relationship you share. The deception was deliberate—and unforgivable.'

'Have you finished? Good, then go back to your cousin and tell her nothing has changed. Make her understand that. The arrangements for the wedding are going ahead as planned.' Her sarcasm was ignored.

'You have not listened to a word I have said,' she gasped. 'Anne is right. Her position here is intolerable. She cannot remain.'

'What do you care for her feelings?' Michael demanded curtly. 'Has she not made your life a misery since you were children? Why pretend she is important to you? Is that not also a deception, mademoiselle?'

From the other side of the room, Nikolai Adashev, unmindful of the wine he had not yet consumed, watched the confrontation between his elder brother and the English girl. Emma knew she had gone too far to back down now. It was all or nothing, and the look in Michael's eyes told her he was not going to allow her to escape unscathed for her impudence.

'My brother has a natural desire to marry and raise a family. I arranged this match with his full approval. Despite her apparent inability to grow up, your cousin has beauty and, I believe, a character worth developing. Once she has adjusted to her new way of life, in a year perhaps, you will not know her. She will be a wife, and, God willing, a mother. The Adashev's have a strong bloodline. She was no idle choice.'

'Selected with as much emotion as you would buy a horse.' Emma was appalled by his words.

'My stables are filled only with thoroughbreds,' came the dry retort.

'If you are so desperate for new blood, why have *you* not married?' she cried. 'As the elder brother do you not also have a responsibility to provide an heir?'

'I fully intend to do just that, but I have only recently selected my future bride. I plan to marry myself within the next year.'

'And have a family produced without love! I pity you! Anne will never agree to such a cold-blooded marriage. If she wishes to leave, then I will help her in any way I can.'

Not until she was half-way up the stairs did Emma realise what she had said. She, a servant, had told the head of the Adashev household it was his duty as well as his brother's, to marry and bring new life into the world. What had come over her? Her own mother had married for love, had been deprived of her husband after five short years, and died without a penny to her name.

What did it matter if Nikolai Adashev liked to drink—or had one leg shorter than the other? He was offering Anne a title and position far above anything she could ever have hoped for in England. She would become the Princess Adasheva, with her own retinue of liveried servants and crested carriages. Her friends would come from the cream of Russian nobility and her children would have an inheritance to be proud of. What was there for her if she returned to her parents? They could not compete with the grand style of living she was being offered now—the massive house—the servants—the wealth—the secure future.

As she reached the landing she was aware of someone coming up behind her. Startled, she turned. Her wrist was clamped by fingers that had the strength of steel in them and she was brought unceremoniously to a halt.

'Now,' Michael Adashev said, tight-lipped. 'We are out of earshot of my brother and the servants, so if you want to continue our little discussion, then your flowery adjectives will be for my ears alone. But I warn you—I have had servants flogged for far less than the insolence you showed me downstairs.'

'We have nothing to say to each other, sir.' Emma tried to twist free, but he held her fast and his grip was so painful she bit her lower lip to stop herself from crying out. 'Before you decide to have me flogged perhaps I should remind you I am responsible for my cousin's safety and well-being to Lord and Lady Tarrant and no-one else. I shall do whatever I think is in her best interests.'

'And you think it is in her best interests to take her home to England? To parents who are almost bankrupt, will never be able to raise a dowry large enough to interest the kind of man Anne wishes to marry. You little fool!' For a moment she thought he was going to shake her. 'Anne's visit to France was her last. Neither her father nor mother had the heart to tell her of their dwindling resources. She spent without consideration of others, and her recklessness has brought them near to ruin. You were aware of this, were you not?'

'I knew they were not as well off as they pretended,' Emma said faintly. She had stopped struggling against his grip. He was too strong, and his words had stunned her. 'Anne—she does not know?'

'Of course not. I promised her parents she would be told nothing. In return for their daughter I paid them a large, a very large sum of money, enough to keep them both for many years to come. Without Anne's extravagance they will be able to live comfortably and continue to keep their circle of friends without anyone knowing what almost happened. I have also promised them, once she is settled, I shall allow them to visit her.'

Emma was silent. She no longer knew what to do. Who was she to pass judgment on Nikolai Adashev's weakness—or the actions of the man before her? She was no-one important.

'I—I will speak to Anne, but I can guarantee nothing,' she faltered. 'I am only a poor relation, after all.' A bitter smile crossed her face. Nineteen years old and poor. But fiercely independent.

'Explain, please. I have grown curious to know why you allow your cousin to treat you no better than a kitchen maid.'

'It is very simple really,' she said. 'My mother married beneath her and was disinherited by her father. All his money, the estate, everything passed directly to Lord Tarrant, Anne's father, when he died. My mother was forced to seek help from them when my father was killed fighting for Charles Stuart, and when she died I was allowed to remain as part of the household.'

'Not part of the family?' Michael queried with a frown.

'Lord Tarrant shared my grandfather's opinion that what my mother had done had brought disgrace upon the family name. They never forgave her. She married for love, you see . . . a Scottish soldier who could give her nothing but his name.'

'And a very special kind of love to make her forsake family and friends—accept the life of an outcast from society,' came the quiet answer.

'And what good did love do her?' Emma demanded. 'My father was killed at Culloden Moor, butchered as he lay wounded on the ground by Cumberland's murdering soldiers. I was only four when it happened. I hardly knew him.'

'And your mother returned to her family?'

'Her father had died the year before Charles Stuart landed in Scotland. She had no-one to turn to except her brother, Lord Tarrant, and she only asked him for help because of me. She had no money, nowhere to live. She begged him for shelter. He took from her the one thing that had kept her alive since my father died . . . her pride. So that I would be clothed and fed and have a roof over my head, she accepted the terrible life he and his wife imposed on her. They never allowed her to forget even for one moment the disgrace she had brought to the Tarrant name, or that she and I survived only because of their Christian charity. She died when I was nine, but life had gone from her long before that. It was a blessed relief.'

'You are very young to be so full of hate.'

'Hate?' Emma shook her head. 'Once I hated them, but not any more. They taught me that emotion is a waste of time and effort. After a while it was no longer important how I felt. I worked in return for my food and clothes, as a scullery-maid, a seamstress, and then as times grew hard for the Tarrants, as Anne's companion and maid. They found it cheaper than engaging a chaperon. They had little money to spend on such extras.'

'Are you saying the Tarrants are extravagant people?' Michael enquired, with a deep frown.

'My cousin has a flair for spending money, but it is not her fault. She has always been given everything she wanted. It is of little consequence though, is it? Soon she will be the responsibility of Prince Nikolai and she has seen by the jewels he sent that he is no pauper. I hope she will be happy, and that she will accept the marriage. Several times she wanted to turn back and go home. She threatened to take passage on the first ship back to England if I did not agree to come with her by coach. Of course we were foolish, but what else could I do? She can be very difficult at times.'

'So it was she and not you who decided to continue alone. She is a pampered child! My brother expects a woman. The miniature he has of her does credit to her beauty, but it does not show what lies beneath the surface.'

'She is only twenty,' Emma protested. 'This is the first time she has ventured further than relatives in France. Prince Nikolai must be patient with her. Surely he understands she is missing her parents and home? The marriage was arranged so quickly it took everyone by surprise. Anne had not been back from Paris a week when she was told she was to be married. I will speak to her now and try to make her see reason, but . . .'

Her wrist was released. She stepped back, rubbing the red marks his fingers had left on her soft skin.

'For her sake—and your own—advise her wisely. If either of you attempt to leave this house, I will have you brought back, by force if necessary. Do I make the position quite clear?

'Perfectly,' Emma replied, ashen-faced. She had no doubt he would carry out the threat without a qualm.

'I am glad we understand each other at last, mademoiselle. I admire your spirit, but not your misguided sense of friendship. Your loyalty is to the House of Adashev now—to me, not your cousin. I trust I will not have cause to remind you of that again in the future.'

He turned on his heel and went downstairs. Emma, still massaging her bruised wrist, watched his tall figure disappear into the drawing-room. He was a tyrant! An ogre! And she had once hoped to have him as a friend!

She expected to find her cousin in a state of hysteria. Instead, when she entered the sitting-room she found Anne seated on a couch, examining a jade statuette.

'Look, Emma.' The scene downstairs might not have happened, she thought in astonishment. Where were the tears, the recriminations, the insults? 'Isn't it beautiful? Who sent it, Irene?'

'The Count and Countess Walinski, Madame. They are close friends of the Prince, your future husband.'

'Wedding presents.' Anne indicated the table in front of her. Emma advanced, wondering if her eyes were playing tricks on her. She saw ornaments of delicate Venetian glass, decanters, crystal glasses, miniatures set in golden frames. A pearl necklace—its lustre took her breath away—and many other items still in their wrappings, lay on the floor. 'This is from the Prince, his wedding present. There, what do you think of that?' Anne held up a necklace. It was almost barbaric in its heavy gold setting, but breathtakingly beautiful, set with two dozen perfectly matched emeralds.

'You—you have accepted it?' Emma was almost afraid to ask.

'Naturally. Oh, you didn't think I meant what I said downstairs, did you? I was angry at that brother . . . daring to pose as a servant just so that he could spy on me. I shall tell Nikolai it was unfair and cruel and that I expect an apology. I am resigned to my fate, such as it is. Nikolai may drink himself to death for all I care, so long as he continues to give me presents like this. Men always drink. Papa does. I dare say he is no worse than anyone else. Well, don't stand there with your mouth hanging open. My clothes have still to be unpacked. I shall wear my white dress down to dinner this evening, the one with the lace fichu. And my emeralds. By the end of dinner I shall have both of them eating out of my hand.'

Emma was sure of that. When Anne set out to charm a man she rarely failed. With her acceptance of the Prince's wedding gift and her decision to stay, the battle was already half won. There was only Michael to be appeased. When he saw her willingness to accept the marriage, he would care little for her reasons. The wedding plans could continue without a hitch and that was all he really cared about.

Emma went into her own room and closed the door behind her. It was a relief to be alone. She needed time to take stock of the situation—her situation. Michael Adashev had made it very clear he expected her to remain as Anne's companion, but answerable for her actions to him and no-one else. She did not care much for that idea.

Everyone in the Adashev household was in the midst of preparations for Christmas. Everyone, that is, except Emma, whose days were spent on her cousin's trousseau. She sewed from morning until night, until her eyes ached and her fingers were too cramped to hold a needle any longer.

She had hardly left the house in the three weeks since her arrival, unlike her cousin, whose days were spent in a whirl of social soirées and dinner parties. As the days slipped by Emma watched her grow more selfish and self-centred. Always she was the main attraction, enjoying the adulation of the titled aristocracy who numbered among Nikolai's friends, giving no thought to her forthcoming marriage or the man who was to be her husband. Emma knew she tolerated him only because he was generous with presents and money. She had only to ask for anything she wanted and he gave willingly, but she made no attempt in return, to get to know him or even to be polite to him.

The maid, Irene, was now her constant companion, following at a respectful distance behind her mistress whenever they went out, sleeping at the foot of the bed like a faithful dog. Emma was made to feel more and more of an outsider. She was sure the woman resented her presence and was doing her utmost to usurp her place at the side of her cousin. Nikolai's constant references to the relationship shared by Emma and Anne made the latter furious, and of late she had begun to retaliate by simply calling Emma her "companion". Once the wedding was over, Emma decided, she would have to look elsewhere for work.

She had seen little of Michael Adashev over the weeks. He seemed to spend a great deal of his time at the Winter Palace with the Grand Duchess Catherine. In the kitchens, the servants talked openly of his close association with the German princess the Czarina had married off to her half-witted nephew, Peter. It was even suggested he was one of her lovers. The cook remarked that the fun-loving Grand Duchess changed her men as frequently as the Czarina changed her dresses, which was often three times a day.

Emma found most of the servants talkative and helpful, especially when they discovered she was prepared to learn their language in order to converse with them and that, despite the fact she was Anne's cousin, she had no illusions of grandeur. Mixing with the "downstairs trash" as Anne described them, did nothing to bridge the widening gulf in their relationship, but for Emma it was a new way of life which grew more attractive with the passing of each day.

The first two weeks Emma was at the house, she took all her meals *en famille*, with Anne, Prince Nikolai and Michael, when he was at home. It was not an arrangement which suited her cousin, and at the beginning of the third week she was told she would in future eat with the rest of the servants. Emma had raised no objection. She felt uncomfortable sitting at the same table as her beautifully-gowned and jewelled cousin, watching Nikolai try to draw her into conversation, and when it failed, turning to the refuge he found in a bottle.

Since her last encounter with Michael, they had exchanged only polite greetings. She wondered if he was happy at the way his plans were progressing. He ignored both Anne's attitude and his brother's drinking habits, and when on one occasion they had begun to quarrel over a dinner party which Anne wanted to attend and Nikolai did not, his face had betrayed no sign. He simply finished his meal and then went to his study, leaving the two of them to continue the argument alone. That time Anne did not get her own way. Nikolai stubbornly refused to go with her and she had flounced out of the room in a rage. Only Irene was allowed near her that night.

Emma discovered that the Adashev servants were well clothed and given a small wage, and for the first time in many years, as she sorted through her meagre, well-worn wardrobe, she resented her lowly position. She had taken for granted, despite Anne's growing dependence on Irene, that she would be allowed to attend the wedding. Now she realised she had nothing suitable to wear and no free time in which to make anything, even if she had had the material available. With a sigh, she returned to her lace-work with such determined concentration that the problem was completely erased from her mind.

The health of the Czarina Elizabeth Petrovna had been slowly declining over the past twelve months, and excessive amounts of wine and entertaining on a grand scale did nothing to slow down the deterioration. From her father, Peter the Great, she had inherited an energetic zest for life. She was a keen horsewoman and a tireless dancer with a passion for balls, often compelling courtiers and attendants to dance continually for hours on end, no matter what age they were or of what rank. She had come to the throne of Russia at the age of thirty-two and it was not very long before a petticoat tyrant replaced the timid, apathetic creature her supporters had once known. Although she abolished the dreaded death penalty, often imposed for minor offences, as soon as she became Czarina banishments took place on a wide scale for the most petty reasons, and the formidable fortress of St Peter and St Paul became the most feared prison in the country, renowned for the many people who disappeared without trace once inside its walls, the inhuman torturing of men and women, and the confinement of the innocent. The new ruler took lovers by the score, usually from the lower classes—footmen, coachmen, lackeys. And yet, despite this, she was a devout churchgoer, observing all the feast days and fasts with equal fervour.

Her irregular way of life took its toll. She was fat and in ill health, and on the eve of Christmas Day she had a stroke. The next afternoon she died, and her nephew, the only grandson of Peter the Great, was proclaimed Peter II, Czar of all the Russias. It was a moment which chilled many hearts.

Emma had heard many conflicting stories about Peter. Some said he was completely mad—a man of thirty-three, with the mentality of a ten-year-old child. Others called him cunning instead of mad, a born soldier like his father, the Duke of Holstein. One thing was not in dispute, his hatred of everything Russian. His aunt had brought him from Holstein when he was fourteen, torn him from friends and family and groomed him methodically to ascend the throne of Russia upon her death. His name was immediately changed from Charles Ulrich to simply Peter, he was forced to convert to the Orthodox faith, and his claim to the throne of Sweden was signed away.

He openly displayed his dislike of anything Russian by spending most of his time at his palace at Oranienbaum, where the regiment of Holstein soldiers he had appointed as his personal guard were billeted. Wearing the red and black uniform of a Holstein officer, he would drill them for hours. When he tired of instructing real fighting men, there were always more imaginary games with his collection of toy soldiers, less dangerous, but just as time-consuming.

The enmity he harboured towards his adopted country also extended to include the wife he had been forced to marry, who, like him, had been separated from her family and home by the Czarina Elizabeth.

The Princess Sophia Augusta of Anhalt-Zerbst, daughter of a Prussian Field-Marshal, had become the Grand Duchess Catherine Alexeevna. The alliance was a disaster from the very beginning. Even after seven years, it was discreetly whispered that the marriage had not been consummated, despite the fact that Catherine had given birth to a son. In the early years, Peter loaded the bed with his toy soldiers and played war games until he fell asleep. Later, he showed affection to every woman except his wife, and surrounded himself deliberately with servants who also disliked her.

After the birth of her son, Paul, whom Peter eventually accepted as his own, but was rumoured to be of doubtful parentage, Catherine began to lead a totally separate life, with her own retinue of servants and friends and a succesion of lovers which she took from among superior army officers. She entertained on the same lavish scale as the Czarina, but at the same time cultivated the friendship of diplomats and ministers of state.

From the moment Peter assumed the crown of Russia, Catherine was aware that his consuming hatred of her had reached a terrifyingly dangerous level. He had already installed his favourite mistress, the Countess Elizabeth Vorontsova, at court, and talked openly of repudiating his unwanted wife at the first suitable opportunity.

Emma was allowed to accompany Anne and Prince Nikolai to the Kazan Cathedral to see the lying-in-state of the late Empress. She knew nothing would ever erase from her mind the magnificence of the spectacle she witnessed that day.

Elizabeth Petrovna lay on a great catafalque, surrounded by tall, lighted candles. She was dressed in a gown of embroidered silver, adorned with lace. Her face had been painted with great care, her hands were smothered in priceless rings and she wore a crown of gold on her head. People wept as they filed past, paying their last respects to the woman who had ruled them for twenty years. Prayers were being chanted in the background for the soul of the departed woman, barely audible at times above the sound of sobbing.

Anne, clad completely in black, found the whole thing boring and uninteresting and took herself off to wait by the main entrance, followed as usual by Irene.

Emma lingered beside Prince Nikolai. The main talking point that morning had been the refusal of the Czar Peter to stand watch over his aunt during the period of lying-in-state, as custom demanded. Instead he remained in his apartments in the Winter Palace, holding riotous supper parties at which his guests were ordered not to wear mourning attire. In contrast, his wife had been to the Cathedral each day for ten days, to keep a constant vigil over the woman who had ruled and overshadowed her life since the first day she set foot on Russian soil.

'Is that the new Czarina?' Emma asked quietly, motioning to the figure shrouded in black veils by Elizabeth's feet.

Nikolai nodded, his gaze intent on the woman who crossed herself with two fingers as was the Russian custom and then prostrated herself before the catafalque. He gave a soft exclamation as a peasant woman, passing behind her, knelt and kissed the hem of her gown before moving away. 'The people feel for her in her grief. She is one with them.'

'But is it not true the old Empress made her life intolerable?'

'She is dead now. All Catherine has to worry about is her husband.'

Something in his tone chilled Emma's heart. So it was true then—the Czar did intend to remove his wife and substitute his mistress in her place.

'I feel very sorry for her,' she murmured as they turned to leave.

'She has many friends, friends who will give their lives for her if necessary,' Nikolai returned.

A man stepped out of the crowd beside them, moving towards the catafalque. Emma heard a greeting pass between him and her companion, turned curiously to watch him approach the prostrate figure of Catherine on the mosaic floor, not recognising him until his features were illuminated by one of the candles. Michael Adashev! He crossed himself, knelt in prayer for a moment and then bent to whisper in the ear of the woman beside him. After a moment she drew herself up, allowed him to take her by the arm and lead her away.

It was the first glimpse Emma had had of Michael for several days. He did not return to the house until the early hours of the next morning. She was closing the curtains in her room before going to bed when she saw a tall, cloaked figure striding across the courtyard which linked the street outside to the back entrance of the Winter Palace. Was he one of the many friends Nikolai had mentioned, willing to die for Catherine should her life be endangered. Or was he, as rumour had it, only one of her many lovers? Emma found the thought disturbing.

She did not attend the funeral in the Kazan, but she heard all about it from the kitchen staff. The new Czar, the all-powerful ruler of Russia, had disgraced himself with the behaviour of a naughty child. He had played the clown throughout the long, pomp-filled funeral procession, altering his pace frequently so that his train bearers had been forced to run to keep up with him. At other times, he slowed down, almost bringing those behind him to a complete standstill. At the solemn Mass he had poked out his tongue at the officiating priest and made jokes with his supporters. Even Anne had remarked upon her return on his childish attitude. He was quite mad, she declared, and unsuitable to manage even his toy soldiers, let alone a country. Emma began to feel sorry for the people of Russia.

The trousseau was finished, every item carefully scrutinised, then pressed and finally packed away in a special trunk, ready to be taken to Malayevka, the Adashev country house where the wedding was now to take place. The last minute change of plans took everyone unawares. Anne's surprise quickly turned to anger when she realised the guest list of well over two hundred people would be cut to less than half if the wedding took place away from St Petersburg.

She insisted they remained in the city, and when Nikolai informed her they were leaving in two days, she stormed back to her room and refused to leave it all that day. Emma was reading in her room when she heard the arrival of a visitor in her cousin's sitting-room and recognised the voice of Michael Adashev. He had not come to argue, he said, or to try and persuade Anne to accept the new arrangements, because he knew that would not be necessary when he explained. He understood her disappointment, but hoped he could alleviate much of it by adding a very special guest to the depleted list, the Czarina Catherine herself.

The strict mourning she was observing made it impossible for her to attend Nikolai's wedding in St Petersburg. People would talk and criticise. But if it was held in the country, then she had agreed to accept the offer he had made for her to spend a few days away from the rigours and demands of court life.

Emma knew nothing now would make Anne refuse the chance of being able to tell everyone in later years how the Czarina of Russia had attended her wedding. Was it Michael who had changed the plans, she wondered? If so, had he really spoken the truth? Or was it an excuse to be alone with Catherine, out of sight of her husband and the spies who surrounded her?

CHAPTER THREE

THAT night Anne went to dine at the house of the Count and Countess Koustev. This engagement provoked the first real argument with Prince Nikolai. He had refused to go with her from the beginning, and he did not change his mind. The house was very quiet. Emma fell asleep by the small porcelain stove which heated her room. When she awoke her supper tray was still perched on her lap. As Prince Michael was out too and Nikolai ate alone in the dining-room, one of the kitchen maids had slipped upstairs with her food. After the strenuous days of working on the trousseau, Emma was only too glad to be alone and able to relax. A clock in the other room chimed eleven times. She yawned and stretched lazily, not really wanting to move, but knowing she should make the effort.

She returned the tray to the kitchen, declined the offer to stay and chat with the housekeeper, and was on her way back upstairs when she heard the sound of shattering glass, followed by a string of abuse that made her wince. She could not understand the Russian words, but the vehemence behind them was clear enough. The drawing-room door was wide open. A footman backed hastily through it, carrying a tray on which were several large pieces of broken glass, and hurried past her without a word. Hesitantly she moved closer until she could see into the room.

Nikolai Adashev was sprawled in a chair. The floor about him was covered in fragments of glass. He was trying in vain to secure a serviette around one hand. She saw the white linen was stained with blood.

'Let me help.' She ran to his side, carefully avoiding

the glass, and knelt by the chair. 'Please let me see, you may have some glass still imbedded in the cuts.'

He had been drinking again, she realised, as he unsteadily thrust his hand out towards her.

'So Anne's little cousin comes to my aid. Aren't you afraid I shall shout at you? The servants don't like me because I shout at them. Do you know that? I might even swear. I do that really well. Like a peasant, your cousin tells me.'

'I know. I heard you a moment ago,' Emma said, frowning at the ugly gash along the back of his wrist and the deep cuts along the palm. 'How did you do this?'

'I smashed a glass with my fingers. I am stronger than I look. Just because I have one leg shorter than the other, that doesn't mean I am not a man!' His voice was harsh with bitterness.

'The wounds are not too deep, but they should be properly cleaned,' she said matter-of-factly. Leaving his side for a moment, she used the bell rope to summon a servant. 'I require hot water and clean towels and bandages,' she told the young girl who stood wide-eyed in the doorway. 'And send someone to clear up the rest of this glass before there is another accident.'

Nikolai chuckled as she turned back to him.

'What a capable young woman you are. Michael was right.' Suddenly he did not sound as drunk as he looked.

'I hardly think a few short days travelling together has made Prince Michael an expert on my character,' Emma returned.

'Michael is an expert in many fields. The managing of our affairs, the running of the country estates, wine, horses, women. He spoke so highly of you I told him perhaps I should marry you instead of Anne.' His eyes considered her as she carefully washed and dried and then bandaged his injury. 'You don't look alarmed. Does the prospect of being saddled with a cripple for the rest of your life not frighten you?'

'As you said yourself, Prince Nikolai, one leg shorter than the other does not make you any less a man.'

Emma's cheeks flooded with colour beneath his close scrutiny. She had always suspected there was more to him than Anne chose to see. She was beginning to believe that his drinking, as well as his inability to communicate with her cousin, stemmed from a feeling of inadequacy because of his leg. Whenever he was with her, however, Emma had found him exceedingly courteous, a totally different person.

'Bring me a large brandy,' Nikolai waved in the direction of the full decanter on the sideboard.

'Do you think you should?' Emma asked cautiously. 'Let me pour you some coffee instead.'

'You sound like my brother,' Nikolai returned with a frown and then his expression softened. 'Very well, little nurse, coffee it shall be. Have some with me and stay a while. I find my own company tedious tonight.'

Emma crossed to the silver samovar at the far end of the dining table and poured coffee into two delicate porcelain cups. She gave one to Nikolai and then perched herself tentatively on the edge of a chair. Until this moment she had given no thought to the way she had taken charge of the situation. She had acted instinctively.

'I cannot stay.' She sipped her coffee. It was black and very strong and she had forgotten to sweeten it. Nikolai drank his without a murmur.

'Why? Are you afraid of me?'

'Good heavens, no!'

'Then it is Anne's displeasure you wish to avoid. She would not take kindly to me conversing with her—companion, would she? Although she finds little time to talk to me herself. There have been moments when I thought I should take a whip to her—show her who is the master.'

'That is the drink talking,' Emma began, and then broke off with a soft exclamation. 'I am sorry. I have no right to speak so freely.'

'Why not? What you say is true. I do drink too much. It gives me the courage I need to face the revulsion I know she feels for me. Do you think I don't know she has only accepted the marriage because I have bought her, with rings and necklaces, and a circle of friends who will make her feel like a queen if I ask it of them, because they are my friends. There is nothing I would not do to keep her with me . . . nothing.'

'I think you are in love with her,' Emma breathed. 'You must tell her . . .'

'I did—tonight, but like you she thought I was too drunk to know what I was saying. I asked her not to go to the Koustev's. I wanted her to dine here with me, just the two of us, so that when we reach Malayevka there would be no more long silences between us, no misunderstandings. She knows how this leg restricts me, yet she expects me to stand to one side and watch her dancing with every man who asks her. It is too much—too much.' His clenched fist thudded onto the arm of his chair with such force that the coffee cup toppled over in its saucer. Emma quickly took it from him and put it, together with her own, safely on the table. Anne loved to dance and she was selfish enough to put her own needs above those of this gentle, misunderstood man who loved her.

'I wish there was something I could do . . .'

'Despite the present estrangement between you, I truly believe you are the only real friend she has,' Nikolai said quietly. 'But there is nothing you can do. The death of the Czarina, inopportune though it is for some people, has given me the chance to leave court for a while and retire to the country. Perhaps there, when we can be alone, Anne and I will be able to resolve our differences.'

'I do hope so,' Emma said sincerely.

'Are you happy here, Emma?' Nikolai asked unexpectedly.

'Why, yes.'

'Anne has hinted that you are not. That you resent Irene taking your place in her favour, and would prefer to find work elsewhere. If that is so, both my brother and

I will help you in any way we can. I am sure there are many people who would be appreciative of your skill with a needle, and your willingness to adapt to new surroundings. Michael has already spoken of a position he considers suitable, as a matter of fact, but he will want to discuss it with you himself, so I will say no more. Forgive me, here I am chattering on when you must be longing for your bed. It is past midnight already.'

'I am rather tired,' Emma admitted, smothering a yawn. She was loath to leave him however. He looked rather young, no more than a year or two older than she was, when in reality she knew he was thirty. And rather lost, as he slid down further into the chair and closed his eyes. The drink was taking effect at last, she thought, quietly getting to her feet.

The sound of voices reached her from the direction of the outer hall. She was almost at the door when it swung open and she found herself face to face with her cousin and Prince Michael. Anne's surprised gaze flickered past her to where Nikolai sat, his eyes tightly closed.

'What are you doing here at this time of night?' Michael asked, drawing off his cloak and gloves. He wore a dark coloured jacket and breeches and an extravagance of white lace at his throat which accentuated the darkness of his skin. Emma saw his eyes slowly scan the room, resting momentarily on the two used coffee cups before returning questioningly to her face.

'Prince Nikolai cut himself on a piece of broken glass. I dressed the wound, that is all,' she answered simply.

'No doubt he was drunk again,' Anne remarked, in a low fierce whisper.

'He has been drinking. He was—was disappointed you did not stay in tonight.'

'He has discussed me with you! One of my own servants!' Her lovely face became indignant. 'You seem to have acquired a knack for accommodating lonely men. Did you share a meal with him too? It's time I sent you back to England where you will be kept in your place.'

Emma grew pale at the cruel reference to the meal she had shared with Michael at the inn during the journey to St Petersburg. More than once since that day it had been intimated that she had been trying to ensure a good position for herself in the Adashev household by being receptive to the elder brother. Anne had stubbornly refused to believe his identity had not been revealed before they reached the house.

Picking up her skirts, Anne brushed past Michael, her eyes like daggers, and flounced from the room.

Crossing to the decanters, Michael poured himself a drink, hesitated and then tipped a small amount of wine into another glass. This one he held out towards his brother's chair. Emma wondered if he had been with Catherine, offering sympathy in her hour of grief.

'You can open your eyes now,' he said, his voice tinged with laughter. 'She has gone.'

Nikolai sat up with a grunt and took the proffered glass.

'Things will be different when we reach Malayevka.' He gave a nod in Emma's direction. 'Thank you for your ministering, little cousin. Don't be upset by her words. If I did not know better I might begin to believe she was jealous to find me in the company of another woman.'

Emma had not even considered that possibility. Could Anne be falling in love with Nikolai—as he had with her?

'I should not have been here . . . I must go to her . . .'

'If you wish,' Michael said, with a shrug, 'but I advise you to leave her to rest. She is overtired and still a little chagrined because the wedding is not to take place here in St Petersburg. Ever since she arrived, she has been telling everyone she meets of the wonderful trousseau being made for her by her personal dressmaker. She has filled them with insatiable curiosity. Now the fact not so many people will be present to admire and congratulate her has hurt her vanity, I think.'

His assessment of Anne's character had been maddeningly accurate from the first time he saw her. He was the only person ever to dare to put into words what Emma thought of her spoilt, ungrateful cousin.

'I'm for my bed,' Nikolai yawned and rose to his feet.

'Your work on the trousseau is finished?' Michael asked as Emma also turned to leave the room.

'Quite finished,' she replied. As was her usefulness to Anne, she thought silently. What had happened tonight had strained their relationship to breaking point. She could go and apologise, but for what? Being on hand to help Prince Nikolai? Or for sharing a few moments with the elder brother who had scarcely spoken two kind words to her since?

'I am looking forward to seeing your handiwork. So, too, is the Czarina, since I told her of your exquisite needlework.'

He had told Catherine about her! What an opportunity that would be if the new Czarina became interested in her work.

'That was kind of you, sir.' Since the day she had discovered his true identity she had been very careful how she addressed him, pointedly erecting a wall between them which made it easier for her to forget that night at the inn when he had been kind. He never made any reference to it, but she saw him smile slightly. 'Once my cousin is married I shall have very little to do. I was thinking perhaps I should look for a position elsewhere, one which would occupy my time more fully.'

Michael's eyes narrowed as he stared across the room at her. He did not register the slightest surprise at her request.

'I am aware of, shall we say, the discord which now exists between you and your cousin, and that I unwittingly instigated it. Should the position not improve at Malayevka, I may be able to offer you alternative employment.'

'Of what nature, sir?' Emma asked, her hopes rising.

'Something which I assure you will be very time consuming, but not unpleasant. We will speak of this again after the wedding. I merely wanted to let you know you need have no fear of being sent back to England.'

'I have no intention of ever going back. I am never going to be treated like a scullion maid again,' Emma said resolutely. 'Wherever I go I will work hard, but for a fair wage, a chance to make something of my life.' She broke off, not wanting him to know how desperate her situation had become. He could not know that she was penniless, dependent on her cousin for everything, including the clothes on her back.

'So you have a taste for freedom, eh? From what I have heard you have already accepted Russia as your new home. Anne would do well to follow your example,' Michael replied with a friendly smile, and Emma felt her heart lurch at the unexpected praise. He was obviously in a good mood. Was it relief at the thought of Anne and Nikolai being married by the end of the week, or the anticipation of being in Catherine's company, out of sight of prying eyes and wagging tongues?

'I am grateful for the chance Lord Tarrant gave me to come to Russia, although at first I must admit I was terribly apprehensive. But I had little choice, had I? You are aware of my background, the way I have lived for years, solely supported by the charity of my own aunt and uncle, treated like a servant, and often an unwanted one, at that.'

'You are headstrong like your mother, are you not? Couple that with the fierce pride of your Scottish father and I believe it possible you would allow your desire for independence to cloud your judgment. I would not like to see that happen. You are a member of my household now and therefore I have naturally assumed responsibility for your welfare. Will you postpone any decision until after the wedding? Then we will talk again in greater detail.'

Emma was so surprised she could only nod. She had certainly not expected help from this quarter. A few more days would make no difference now she had made up her mind to leave her cousin's service, and with his circle of influential friends and acquaintances she stood the chance of finding herself a well paid and secure position. A great weight was lifted from her mind. She ran up the stairs to her room as if her feet had suddenly grown wings.

The Adashev estates were situated in the heart of the country, between the Czar's palace at Oranienbaum and the Summer Palace at Peterhof. From the troika which conveyed her across the frozen countryside, securely wrapped in furs to keep out the intense December cold, Emma eagerly awaited her first sight of the house. Prince Nikolai and Anne were in the troika some yards ahead, with Michael himself controlling the three high-stepping black horses. Only a skeleton staff had been left behind in the city. The remainder of the servants and masses of luggage had already travelled ahead.

They had just passed through a village of small log houses with thatched roofs of mud and straw. It was surrounded by a dense forest of tall, snow-laden pine and birch trees, where the sun barely penetrated.

Unexpectedly the foliage began to thin out. The troikas sped along a long, wide driveway and were brought to a halt amid a flurry of loose snow in front of a large, sprawling red brick house, with many outhouses and stables alongside it. A flight of stairs led up to a massive pair of oak doors, set with wrought ironwork. Chiselled into the stone archway above them, Emma saw the familiar stag's head surmounted by a circlet of leaves—the Adashev coat-of-arms.

Prince Nikolai quickly escorted Anne inside, but Emma lingered for a while on the steps, her cheeks glowing from a biting wind as her eyes swept the desolate countryside around her. She had been only four years old when her father had died, but she had one clear recollection of riding across countryside not unlike this, cradled in his arms on the back of a big horse. When she had spoken of it to her mother some years later she had been told they had been riding over Culloden Moor. It had been one short week before that bleak, mist-shrouded moor had been covered with dead and dying Highlanders, the flower of Bonnie Prince Charlie's army. She shivered and turned towards the door—and found Michael Adashev standing there, watching her.

'When the first Spring flowers creep from the cold earth and push their way towards the sun, this is a very different place,' he said quietly.

'I think it is quite beautiful now,' Emma returned quickly, not wanting him to think she had disliked his house on sight.

'Then why did you shiver? A painful memory perhaps—from the past?'

She nodded, but offered no explanation.

'Come inside and get warm.' He turned back into the house and she followed, past gleaming, freshly-polished furniture, servants hurrying to and fro with luggage and fresh linen for the guests, into a long, low room dominated by a huge chasm of a fireplace.

Anne and Nikolai sat warming themselves before the inviting flames leaping up from enormous logs, piled three and four high in the hearth. Colourful tapestries hung from the walls and there were Persian carpets on the marble floors. Emma saw that her cousin was smiling as she studied her surroundings. The house and the wealth it displayed was obviously once again to her satisfaction.

A petite, brown-haired girl in her teens detached herself from their side as Emma hovered hesitantly in the doorway and came towards her with a shy smile. Her velvet dress was trimmed with sable fur and diamonds sparkled around her neck and on the hand she held out towards the newcomer. Emma wondered why such an attractive girl had chosen a life of seclusion in the country instead of the court life in St Petersburg.

'You have to be Emma. From Michael's description I would have known you anywhere. I am Maritza Adasheva.' She had Nikolai's gentle voice, but Michael's features. 'Welcome to Malayevka. I have been looking forward to your arrival.' Her eyes were friendly, blue like those of Michael, but lacking their intensity.

'Forgive me. I didn't recognise you!' Those were the words Michael had spoken to Emma when they met at the inn—yet she knew they had never encountered each other before. And now his sister welcomed her as a guest instead of a member of her brother's household!

A servant took Emma's cloak. She followed him to the fire. A table beside it was laid with silver platters containing fruit and sugared biscuits and a samovar of hot chocolate. She was given a cup which she sipped gratefully, feeling it slowly bring back some feeling to her frozen bones.

Maritza sat on the sofa beside Nikolai and launched into an excited barrage of questions about the life at court, the funeral of the Empress, and finally, the wedding of Nikolai and Anne Tarrant. As she talked it became clear to Emma that she had not been in St Petersburg for many months, not since the early summer, in fact.

'I am so looking forward to coming back to St Petersburg. It is lonely here, and dull.' Her tiny mouth drooped, and from beneath long lashes she cast a speculative glance in the direction of her elder brother.

'The Czarina could hardly appear at a wedding when she has ordered the whole of her court to go into a strict period of mourning,' Michael replied, acknowledging her silent question. 'The wedding will take place here the day after tomorrow and that is when she will arrive. I need hardly remind you, as hostess you will be responsible for ensuring she is provided with every comfort. We will have many other guests who will also require your attention. You will not find the next few days dull, little sister, I assure you.'

'The Czarina here!' Maritza gasped. 'That's wonderful. Anne, how can you sit there so calmly? I would be a nervous wreck if Catherine herself was to be present at my wedding. How many guests are coming, Michael? Why didn't you send word ahead? Two days! But that is no time at all! We shall never be ready.'

'Gently, little one, I was only teasing. Everything has been arranged,' Michael said, with a soft chuckle. He reached out and touched her flushed cheek affectionately. 'All you have to do is act the graceful hostess when she arrives and that you will do very well. I know I shall be proud of you. Now, why don't you show Anne to her rooms? It is time the two of you became properly acquainted.'

Michael stepped away from the fire as Emma picked up her cloak and prepared to follow them.

'It is good to be home again, eh, Nikolai?' he murmured, his hand resting for a moment on his brother's shoulder. 'To be able to relax . . .'

'My brother's idea of relaxation is to spend all day in the saddle touring the estate. Up at dawn—home at dusk,' Nikolai said, looking at Emma. 'Do you ride, little cousin?'

He had addressed her in this fashion since the night she had bandaged his injured hand, even in the presence of her cousin who missed no opportunity to accuse Emma of 'forgetting her place'.

'I never had time to learn,' she confessed. It was something she had always longed to do.

'We must remedy that as soon as the wedding is over. Maritza rides like the wind. She will teach you,' Michael interposed. 'Are you looking forward to seeing the results of all your hard work?'

'I was given to understand you would not be present at the wedding.'

Nikolai's softly spoken words hit Emma like a clenched fist. So Anne had already taken precautions against the embarrassment of having her poor relation mixing with her new elite circle of friends. She did not know what to say, how to extricate herself from the humiliation which came crashing down on her head. Once again Anne had reminded her cruelly, deliberately, of her role in life. She could plead illness, but both men could see she was in good health.

Michael's eyes narrowed at her continued silence. He looked at his brother enquiringly.

'Is there something I have not been told?'

'Anne has conveyed to me Emma's wish to absent herself from the celebrations altogether,' his brother replied. 'She gave no reason.'

Anne would not consider it necessary, Emma thought, the colour receding from her cheeks under Michael's scrutiny.

'Is this your decision—or Anne's?' he demanded.

'Since I arrived in Russia, both you and Prince Nikolai have taken into account my relationship with Anne—that I am not only her companion, but her cousin. I thank you for that kindness, but in England I was treated quite differently. You know that. My position over the past weeks has grown unbearable because of your acceptance . . .' Emma's grey eyes pleaded with Michael not to force the issue. She addressed herself to him rather than his brother, knowing he was the one who ruled the house, made all the decisions. When she had told him of her background, she had not told him she was dependent on Anne, even for the clothes on her back. The last vestige of pride she possessed forbade her to admit it. He had eyes of his own; surely he must understand her reason for confirming the lie forced upon her now. 'In my opinion—I—I have no place at her wedding. I would prefer not to attend.'

'When it becomes necessary to remind you of your place, mademoiselle, then I will be the one to do so,' Michael answered slowly. 'Very well. We will not speak of this again.'

'Thank you. If you will excuse me, I must go and make sure everything has arrived safely.'

It took Emma the rest of the day to supervise the unpacking of the vast array of clothes Anne had accumulated since her arrival in St Petersburg. She personally unwrapped the precious trousseau and hung it away in the massive carved wardrobes before turning her attention to the many wedding presents which filled four wooden crates.

It was growing dark by the time she thought of unpacking her own meagre belongings, only to discover her battered trunk was nowhere to be seen.

Anne was reclining on a couch in the bedroom, wrapped in a fur-trimmed pelisse, watching Irene lay out a selection of gowns from which she would choose a suitable one for that evening. Maritza sat in a nearby chair.

'The green satin with the fichu of white lace will do nicely.'

She looked across the room with a frown as Emma began opening closet doors, peering behind the large items of furniture. 'What are you doing?'

'My things—I can't find them. I thought they had been left in my room.' She was referring to the small adjoining antechamber which she had naturally assumed would be hers.

'Your room!' Anne echoed, her mouth tightening in annoyance. The cold tone told Emma matters had come to a head.

She sighed. She was tired and did not want another unpleasant scene—especially in front of the Princess Maritza.

'Perhaps Irene will show me where I am to sleep then,' she said patiently. Some attic probably. Out of sight and out of mind.

'You can see she is busy. Find one of the other servants. I shall not need you again tonight. You may do as you please.'

How generous, Emma thought bitterly. She knew it was useless to protest over the new arrangements and left the room without another word. She eventually found her room. It was at the top of the house and contained only the bare essentials—an iron bed, a chest of drawers and a marble-topped washstand. The stove looked as if it had not been alight for years.

For a moment she stood in the doorway surveying her pitiful surroundings and remembering the comfortable room in St Petersburg. She wanted to cry, then, pulling herself together, she began to unpack. It was no worse than the tiny cold attic room in London, and she had survived that for many years. Brighter prospects lay ahead—if she was patient.

Her first encounter with Michael, when she had challenged his authority, believing as she did then that he was a servant himself, had made her remember how strong-willed she had been as a child—the independent nature which had earned her scorn and rebuke, the quick temper she had learned to control. He had awakened these things in her again. Never, she silently vowed to herself, never would she allow anyone to treat her like dirt again!

She awoke later than usual in the morning and dressed in a frantic haste, wondering why Irene had not been sent to rouse her from her bed. The wedding was only a day away and there was a lot to do. She was met with frosty stares from both her cousin, and the maid hovering at her elbow as she lay in bed eating her breakfast. She looked every inch the grand lady, Emma thought, as she apologised for her lateness.

'You will be trying on the wedding dress this morning? I am sure that no alterations will be necessary, but perhaps you would like to make sure.'

'Have I not made myself clear, Emma?' Anne interrupted coldly. 'Irene is capable of taking care of me today, tomorrow, and for years to come. She is quite efficient for a country woman and far less clumsy with my hair than you were. You do not look surprised? No, I thought not. I know you have already decided to find another position, but if you think you have any influence over Nikolai, you are wrong. He will not help you, nor his brother. In fact when I discussed you with Michael, he agreed it would be better if you left my service immediately. I think Moscow would suit you.'

'Moscow,' Emma repeated in a hollow voice. She had not dreamed she would not have a choice as to where she worked next. 'But I like St Petersburg. I could easily find work there as a seamstress or a governess.'

She ignored the pointed remark about Nikolai, accustomed now to Anne's spiteful comments on the fact he seemed more taken with Emma's company than that of his future wife.

'And have everyone asking me, the Princess Adasheva, how my poor cousin is getting on? I would die of shame. No, you will be sent to Moscow—or back to England. The choice is yours.'

'Far enough not to do any damage.' Emma went white with anger. 'You are a fool, Anne. I do not want to bask in your limelight. These past few weeks have made me want to get as far away from you as possible. As for Prince Nikolai, he likes my company because he can talk to me—that is more than he can say for you. The poor man loves you and you use his feelings without one iota of conscience . . .'

'How dare you!' Anne leapt from the bed. The breakfast tray and its contents crashed to the floor. Before Emma could move she had swung back her hand and slapped her soundly across both cheeks. 'Get out. I never want you near me again. Do you understand?'

The blows were so savage that they rocked Emma on her feet and brought tears rushing to her eyes. She reeled blindly towards the door and found it was already open. Maritza stood on the threshold, a horrified expression on her pretty features.

'Excuse me, Princess,' Emma faltered.

'Emma! I have been looking for you. My brother Michael wishes to speak with you in his study in ten minutes.'

Michael! He was the last person Emma wanted to see. He probably intended to tell her he had found work for her in Moscow, where no-one knew her, and she would not be connected with the respectable name of Adashev. Ignoring the other girl, she ran downstairs, through the servants quarters and out into the garden. She stopped only when forced to do so by lack of breath. Beneath a tall birch tree she paused and leaned weakly against the gnarled trunk, giving way to a flood of tears, which, when they receded, left her drained of all the little dreams she had begun to harbour . . . empty and without hope.

A flurry of snow cascaded down on her as the wind stirred the branches overhead. She shivered in the icy morning air. Her thin dress was no protection against a bone-chilling wind and she turned back towards the house. With luck she could reach her room without being seen and plied with awkward questions as to the reason for her tear-streaked face.

She did not see—or hear—the horse which was suddenly upon her and she was forced to throw herself to one side to avoid being run down. As she lay in the snow, dazed and trembling with both cold and fear, she heard a string of Russian oaths and the next moment Michael Adashev was lifting her to her feet, his features grey with shock.

'Are you hurt? Devil take you, girl—what are you doing outside without protection?' His fingers probed her arms and shoulders for some sign of injury, ignoring her protests that she was unhurt uttered between chattering teeth. He brushed snow from her hair and clothes, pulled off the heavy fur jacket he wore and wrapped it securely about her.

'Th-thank you. I—I am sorry . . . I didn't see you . . .'

'The fault was mine. The snow muffled the animal's approach and I was deep in thought,' Michael answered. His fingers lightly touched her wet cheeks. 'You have been crying. You will ride back with me and tell me what is wrong.'

His tone belied argument. She was lifted on to the back of his black stallion as if she weighed no more than a feather. As he swung himself up behind her she felt herself instantly tense at the contact of his hard, masculine body against hers. She found him too attractive by far, and it was becoming increasingly difficult to ignore the fact. The sooner she went away the better.

As Michael guided the horse over the snow-covered

ground, Emma found herself remembering once again the day she had ridden with her father on Culloden Moor. It was the first and only time she had been on a horse. She was a little girl no longer, but a grown woman, and there was no way she could look on Michael Adashev as a father figure.

Perhaps it was the intense cold or the fact she had eaten nothing yet, probably a mixture of both she realised later on, but when Michael lifted her down, her legs had no strength in them and, but for the support of his strong arms, she would have fallen. Without a word he picked her up and carried her into the house. Jan appeared as he deposited her on a couch in the drawing-room, and without being given any orders went directly to a cut-glass decanter and filled two glasses with dark red wine.

'Good lad.' Michael took one and held it to Emma's lips. She tried to push it away, afraid it would go straight to her head on an empty stomach, but he insisted and she gave in and drank it. It felt like fire as it went down her throat, but was instantly warming.

Jan handed his master his glass. Michael stepped back and perched himself on the edge of the table, his eyes never leaving Emma's white face as he drank. The clothes he wore today were familiar to her—hide trousers and a leather doublet and knee-length leather boots. This was the Michael she had met at the inn. She sensed he was more at ease dressed this way instead of in the rich attire it was necessary to don for court appearances. He wore only one item of jewellery—a heavy ring bearing his family crest on his left hand. The blue eyes considering her held a question. He was still waiting to know why she had been so foolish as to go outside, she realised. She had confided in him once, trusted him. But she was loath to do so again. She was vulnerable just now, desperately needing a friend. But not him.

'Well,' he said at length.

'There is nothing to tell,' Emma said quietly. 'I—I think the preparations for the wedding must have been too much for me. I suddenly found myself wanting to cry.'

It was the lamest of excuses and she saw immediately that he did not believe her. He nodded briefly in Jan's direction and they were left alone.

'Preparations in which you are no longer involved, from what I have been told. Has Anne dismissed you?'

Mutely Emma nodded and he gave an annoyed frown.

'She will learn, in time, that one does not discard true friends. But surely this was not unexpected. Things have been growing more difficult between you. You said so yourself only yesterday.'

'Yes . . . but the change in her . . . almost overnight . . . as if we had never shared anything together.'

'Drink! You look as if you are about to faint,' Michael said as he refilled both their glasses. 'Tomorrow she will be Nikolai's responsibility—not yours or mine. It is time you gave a little thought to yourself and what you want to do.'

'Has that not already been decided for me?' Emma asked, her tone growing apprehensive. 'Am I not to be sent to Moscow, far enough away from everyone for my name never to be linked with hers again.'

Michael's mouth tightened at her words.

'So that is what she told you. And her reasons?'

'With Irene to look after her she no longer needs me. And the thought of me working in St Petersburg does not appeal to her.'

'I think also she is a little jealous of the way Nikolai has taken to you. You and he have become friends, have you not?'

'You do not approve?'

'He is a grown man, his personal life is none of my affair, provided it does nothing to discredit our name. However, I would not like to see your cousin continually using this as an excuse to continue this antagonism between you.'

'I am to be sent away then.' What other alternative was there?

'Not unless you wish it. I had not intended to speak of this matter again until after the wedding, but Anne's action has made it necessary. I have a position in mind for you, one I think you will find a challenge. My sister is lonely, she needs the company of some level-headed person of her own age. I think you are a most suitable choice.'

'Me!' Emma's eyes widened in amazement. 'But surely she has many friends . . .'

'Maritza has formed an attachment . . . a liaison with someone totally unsuitable.'

'A man?'

'Of course,' he returned disapprovingly.

'Which is why she is here at Malayevka and not at court.'

'How very astute of you. Yes, that is the reason. If she was at court, among her friends, friends who I am led to believe think as she does, then I would be unable to keep track of her movements. If she has a companion of my choice, I shall know exactly where she is every minute of the day—and who she sees.'

'You want me to spy on her! What a monstrous idea.' Emma shook her head. What little she had seen of Maritza she had liked. Nothing would induce her to stay in order to watch over her in such a fashion. 'I am sorry, Prince Michael, I cannot accept your offer.'

'The alternative is to return to England, and that I know you are against, or to go to Moscow, to a strange family. Don't give me an answer now, think about it. Chaperon Maritza for the next few days until all the excitement is over. Get to know her before you make up your mind.'

The offer was tempting, Emma could not deny that.

'It is out of the question.'

'Why? Because your pride will not allow you to admit to me you have no decent clothes in which to appear at your cousin's wedding?'

'As you are aware of my reason for refusing, I see no reason to discuss the matter further.' Emma sat up, removing the heavy jacket he had placed around her shoulders outside, averting her gaze so that he would not see the rush of fresh tears his words had brought to her eyes.

'The matter has been dealt with. Did you think I would subject you to such an ordeal? As soon as Maritza told me what had happened concerning your room, I realised other arrangements were necessary and had to be made quickly. I hope you will find your new accommodation more comfortable. As for clothes—that problem too has been taken care of. I give the orders in this house, mademoiselle—not Anne. Her behaviour is inexcusable.'

'I was very rude to her,' Emma admitted.

'With good reason, according to my sister, who is not in the habit of exaggerating. Well, are you going to be a sensible young woman?'

'Do I really have a choice?'

'Yes. Not such a pleasant one perhaps, but a choice. It is up to you. Come now, is my suggestion really too intolerable even to consider? Do you honestly believe you would be welcomed by your aunt and uncle if you returned to them? Is Moscow more inviting than here—than St Petersburg? I hope you will not only be Maritza's companion, but her friend, advisor . . .'

'Then my life will be little different than with my cousin.'

'So long as you follow my instructions to the letter, you will be treated well. After tomorrow you will become part of the family, after all, whether it is to your liking or not. Already I believe Maritza looks on you as a friend. Believe me, my sister is very important to me.'

'Yet you deny her happiness by depriving her of the man she finds attractive.' Part of the Adashev family . . . how would Anne receive that suggestion?

'In this case I am the best judge of what is best for her. She is a child where love is concerned. It is an infatuation, nothing more. It will pass.'

'And if it does not?'

Michael stared down at one booted leg crossed casually over the other for a long moment before he lifted his head to ask:

'Have you ever been in love, Emma?'

She coloured at the use of her christian name. It was the first time he had ever used it.

'No.'

'Then please permit someone more knowledgeable than yourself to decide what is the best course of action. Do you feel strong enough to walk now? Good. Wait while I send for someone to take you upstairs. You will go straight to bed with some warm milk.'

Michael rang for a servant. When one of the young maids appeared he gave instructions Emma was to be put to bed and all her meals that day were to be served in her room. Before she had a chance to thank him, he had picked up his jacket and left her.

CHAPTER FOUR

EMMA found that she had been given a pleasant sitting-room and bedroom on the same floor as her cousin, but at the end of the long corridor, with Maritza's rooms between them. Her belongings had been brought from the attic and put away, and someone had lit the enamelled stove. The maid left Emma to get undressed, returning, just as she was climbing into bed, with a glass of warm milk, spiced with something which smelled suspiciously like brandy. Emma drank every drop and slept soundly for several hours.

She was awakened late in the afternoon by the noise of a carriage arriving outside and the sound of voices. Pulling on a wrap, she hurried to the window. Not one carriage, but three were in the courtyard below. Nikolai Adashev and Michael were greeting the new arrivals with smiles and handshakes and servants were busy unloading boxes and cases. Wedding guests, Emma thought, prepared to stay for more than just a few days by the look of all that luggage.

She was seated by the fire, working on a piece of lace which she hoped to use on one of Anne's discarded dresses, when there was a knock on the door.

'Come in.' Had Anne sent Irene to summon her back to apologise for the ugly scene that morning?

'I hope I am not disturbing you, but when Michael told me how he had almost run you down with that great brute of a horse of his, I had to come and make sure you were all right.' Maritza appeared. Her arms were full of clothes. 'Have you slept at all? Have you eaten?'

'Thank you, Princess, I have done both. It was kind of you to think of me,' Emma answered, her heart warming towards the other girl for her kind gesture.

'Please call me Maritza. You are almost one of the family, after all, whatever Anne chooses to think. Michael has spoken to you about staying with us. He says you are not leaving until after the wedding—if at all. I am glad. It is so dull here, I shall enjoy the company. He said I could teach you to ride if you wanted to.'

'I should like that, although I very much doubt if I shall be able to stay more than five minutes on the horse's back. I have no sense of balance,' Emma said with a soft laugh.

'Nonsense, I shall make a fine horsewoman out of you and then you will be able to hunt with us and I shall show you the countryside around Malayevka. It is very beautiful, even in Winter.' Maritza carefully spread the dresses she was holding across the bottom of the bed. One was velvet, the other fine embroidered watered silk. Emma looked at them in silence, her cheeks beginning to burn at the implication of the action. 'Do not be offended, Emma, please. It was not my intention to embarrass you, but you must have something nice to wear tomorrow. Please change your mind and come with me to the wedding.'

To be able to mingle with the guests, drink the health of her cousin in champagne, wearing one of those exquisite creations. Why not? And why should she not accept Michael's offer? She would become a respected member of his household wth money of her own, decent clothes. A chance to remember too that she had a heritage. He was offering her the very thing she yearned for—her independence.

'I have offended you,' Maritza said contritely.

'No—indeed you have not. I—I will come. Thank you for making it possible for me to hold up my head in front of all your friends.'

'How proud you English are—almost as proud as we Russians. I must go now. I have to make sure my guests are comfortable. I will tell Michael the good news. I know he will be pleased.' She paused in the doorway, a mischievous smile lighting up her features. 'You have made quite an impression on both my brothers, do you know that, Emma? Nikolai has begun to think of you as one of the family already, and Michael . . . he has not been the same since he first saw you. As for me—I like you, Emma Fraser. I hope you will stay with us for a long, long time and that you will become my friend. I have need of one, believe me.'

She was gone before Emma could question her. If she stayed, she knew they would be friends, close friends. The seeds of that unselfish relationship had already been sown. It was in that instant Emma decided to accept the position as Maritza's companion. She would tell Michael at the wedding the next day.

Slowly Emma pirouetted before the large gilt-framed mirror on the bedroom wall, her cheeks flushed with excitement as she surveyed her reflection. Maritza's dress, and the nimble hands of her personal maid Katya in dressing the long black hair, had brought about a transformation from an insignificant little mouse to a graceful swan.

She turned again, scrutinising herself from every angle as she had often seen her cousin do. Not only did she look different, but she felt it too. The girl staring back at her from the mirror looked every inch a lady—graceful—elegant—radiating confidence. The gown of watered silk had needed only a tiny alteration to the waist; now it fitted like a glove. The low neckline had been modified with the addition of a beautiful white lace fichu. The pale yellow material embroidered with delicate, hand-sewn flowers, was not too great a contrast against her pale skin and showed off to perfection her hair which Katya had brushed until it shone and then twisted into heavy curls secured on the top of Emma's head with dozens of carefully concealed pins. Emma had, for years, managed Anne's hair perfectly well, but when it came to doing her own she had found it a hopeless task, and had been at her wits end when Katya appeared, sent by Maritza to help in any way she could.

She was aware of heads turning to watch her as she descended the stairs. She acknowledged with a shy smile someone who spoke to her and pretended not to notice the curious stares of many others. To her relief Maritza came threading her way through the guests hovering by the chapel door and led her inside. Her dress was white satin, threaded with silver and lavished with white fur. Around her neck she wore the biggest sapphire Emma had ever seen. It was easy to see why Michael was so intent on keeping a strict watch on her, Emma thought. At court she would be sought after by many eligible young men—and those who did not fall into that category also.

'Emma you look lovely. How did Michael know that colour would suit you so well?'

'He—he said that?' Emma asked disbelievingly.

'He selected both gowns, but he said you would prefer the yellow.'

'It is my favourite colour, but how could he know such a thing?'

'There are times when I think my brother has a talent for reading minds.'

Emma followed her into one of the front pews, trembling a little at the excitement of the occasion. The chapel was full of sumptuously dressed men and women. Many, she suspected, were titled aristocracy and here was she, Emma Fraser, in a position of importance beside Princess Maritza Adasheva as if she was an honoured guest herself.

The air was heavy with the heady perfumes of incense. The gold altar cloth and many priceless icons placed around, glittered in the light of hundreds of candles, competing to outshine the jewellery on display.

How had Michael known she would decide to wear the yellow silk? The question nagged at Emma's brain. At last she could contain her curiosity no longer and bending close to Maritza whispered:

'How did Prince Michael describe me to you?'

'I was wondering when you would ask me that,' the girl replied, her eyes sparkling with amusement. 'He told me he had seen a girl who was the fairest of the fair, with eyes reminiscent of storm clouds on a summer's day, and the bearing of a queen. In Russia only someone with hair as black as yours can be described as fair. It is the biggest compliment any Russian man could ever pay you. Why even the Empress Elizabeth used to dye her hair and eyebrows jet black so that she would appear more beautiful than any other woman at court. Oh, by the way, I remember now. He said you were wearing yellow that day too.'

'But that isn't true . . . when we first met I was . . .' Emma's voice trailed off into a stunned silence.

The day he first saw her, were the words Maritza used. Not the day they first met at the inn. Emma had possessed only one yellow dress in her life and it had once belonged to her mother. She had worn it when she accompanied Anne to France and her duties as a companion had turned into those of a chaperon. In France! But that was where Michael had first set eyes on her cousin and chosen her as his brother's bride! France, not the miserable inn outside St Petersburg. That explained how he had identified her so easily. She could hardly believe it! She had been noticed by a Prince.

Anne looked beautiful in her gown of white brocade striped with cream. The sleeves had triple cuffs of embroidered muslin and the underskirt was a mass of cream lace. The head-dress—a present from Nikolai to his bride, and a family heirloom—was breathtaking. It fell gracefully to Anne's shoulders and then swept out behind her in a magnificent train that was all of six feet long. She had never looked lovelier. This was her moment—and she knew how to use it to full advantage. Every movement, every seemingly shy look stolen from beneath lowered eyes at the guests, was intended to engage their good affections. Emma had seen such coquettish flattery many times before. She wondered what thoughts lay behind that charming smile as she took the hand Nikolai extended and allowed him to lead her towards the door.

Unexpectedly Anne looked towards the pew where she stood, obviously to acknowledge Maritza, Emma realised, and caught sight of her. Her step faltered as astonishment, bewilderment, then anger flashed into her eyes. Emma was aware of Nikolai's hand tightening over Anne's, urging her on past the crowded pews. No, Emma thought, she would not be sorry she had chosen to leave her cousin's service.

'She looks lovely,' Maritza breathed as they followed at a distance. 'You should have seen the look on the face of Madame Thérèse when she saw Anne's gown. She was green with envy.'

'Madame Thérèse?' Emma queried.

'My French dressmaker. She thinks she is the best in the world, because she has made clothes for the late Empress. Now she has been shown different. You have a great talent, Emma, and it will be much in demand. Would you mind if some of my friends asked you to make gowns for them?'

'I should be very pleased, and honoured they think me capable.' Emma veiled the delight in her expression. It was all too good to be true. Soon she might have enough money and time to begin making a fine wardrobe of her own.

'I told you the English are not only reserved, but modest.' Michael's amused tones sounded behind them as they entered the ballroom where a cold buffet had been laid and liveried footmen hovered by the door with trays of ice-cold champagne.

Emma felt her cheeks burn at the undercurrent of mockery she heard there. He knew the truth. She threw back her head and stared up into his dark features challengingly, and was surprised to see no mockery in the eyes which swept over her, taking in every detail of her appearance, from the tip of her shining black curls to the embroidered silk shoes on her feet.

'I chose well,' he said, with a smile at his sister.

'Michael often advises me on my own clothes,' Maritza admitted, accepting the glass of champagne he was holding out to her. 'He knew what would suit you and he was right. He has good taste, has he not, Emma?'

Emma thought it wiser not to voice her own opinion on that point.

'Not all men are blind to the beauty which surrounds them,' Michael returned and she knew he had not expected an answer. 'Would you care for some champagne, Emma?'

'A small glass, please.'

Now she had been accepted as part of the family because she was Anne's cousin, he could of course refer to her in any way he chose, she thought, and it should not matter to her. If only he did not make her name sound so nice—so special.

She bent her head low over the glass so that neither of them should see the confusion which came flooding into her cheeks. She was still nothing more than his sister's companion, yet here she was, beginning to have the same illusions of grandeur as she had previously condemned in her cousin. She was in no position—improved though it was—to harbour ideas above her station. He was being kind. Nothing more.

It was the dress, she decided, the feel of silk against her skin, the memory of the image that had faced her from the looking-glass, which made her feel so different.

'I thought the Czarina might have been here by now,' Maritza said after a careful study of everyone in the room, and her tone held disappointment.

'Patience, my sister, she will be here. It has been snowing steadily for the past twenty-four hours and you know what that will have done to the roads. I have a dozen men out clearing the way. You do have other guests, remember. Do you not think it time to mingle a little,' Michael suggested.

'Yes, I suppose you are right. You will tell me when she comes, won't you?'

'My dear girl, when Catherine walks into the room

everyone will know it,' her brother chuckled, and Maritza left them.

Emma felt her heart lurch unsteadily at the intimate way he referred to the Czar's wife. It seemed to confirm the rumours she had heard concerning their relationship. The Czarina's lover? Yes, he was handsome enough to attract her attention, she thought, as her eyes dwelt on the dark, enigmatic features, and, she suspected, man enough to hold his own against other favourites. She found it hard to imagine Michael Adashev in love, allowing himself to be ruled by emotion. He always seemed to be so much in command, not only of himself, but others. He ruled his household with a firm hand and although she had never heard a bad word spoken against him, Emma was certain that, should it become necessary, it was in his nature to be ruthless and unyielding in his attitude—even cruel!

'I would say you have fully recovered from our unfortunate encounter yesterday.' His gaze was intent on her face and she realised that she had been staring at him for some considerable time, lost in the intensity of her own thoughts.

'Yes, I have. It was very foolish of me to run out of the house the way I did. I hope you do not think I am always such a scatterbrain. It was just that . . .' Her voice trailed off as he waved aside her attempt to apologise.

'If I did, do you think I would have asked you to remain as Maritza's companion? Under the circumstances which prevailed I understand, and I think it best if we forget the entire incident.'

At the far end of the room half a dozen long tables had been laid with the most mouth-watering array of food she had ever seen in her life. Servants were serving guests with slices of roast grouse stuffed with truffles, or succulent roast sucking-pig, or chicken. There was caviar and wafer-thin pancakes filled with cream. Not a glass remained empty for longer than a minute. The champagne flowed like water.

'You are hungry perhaps?' Michael asked. 'Come, we will see what there is.'

She was taken by the arm and led towards the tables. Emma felt dozens of pairs of eyes boring into her back, all expressing the same silent question as to the identity of the girl in the yellow dress at the side of Michael Adashev.

She was handed a plate which held slices of chicken and sucking-pig, side by side, together with a silver fork bearing the Adashev coat-of-arms. She looked down at it for a long moment as it reminded her she was not really a guest, but a paid servant. Then, with a soft sigh, she took a mouthful of chicken. It was too tempting to refuse and she was very hungry, having been too nervous to eat anything since the night before.

'You have made this a day for Anne to remember all her life,' she said quietly, wondering if her cousin had had the good maners to thank those concerned for the tremendous efforts made on her behalf.

'And for you?'

'Yes, for me too,' she admitted. 'Without your understanding, and Maritza's great kindness, I should not be here. I think you know I am very grateful.'

'Gratitude is the last thing I want from anyone,' Michael replied, a frown deepening his dark brows. 'Loyalty is what I ask, demand, from those I employ. You have had ample time to consider my offer. I would like an answer.'

It was time to make the decision which would link her life with the House of Adashev, Emma thought. No, if she was honest with herself, Maritza was not the reason she would be accepting his offer, nor the independence which would accompany such a position, not even the total change of status involved. The real reason stood at her side, blue eyes narrowing a fraction impatiently at her hesitation.

'I accept your offer, Prince Michael.'

'Now you are acting with the good sense you showed when we first met at that god-forsaken inn.'

'At the inn, sir?' Emma's gaze locked with his and a smile touched her lips. 'Surely you are mistaken. That was the second time.'

'You have been talking to Maritza,' he said. Her comment aroused no other remark.

'She had no idea I was unaware of that other time.'

'First impressions are always the most important. I prefer to make an appraisal when the person concerned is unaware, as you were, that they are under scrutiny. One can learn a great deal from using the eyes instead of the tongue. You may find it wise to remember that, now you are to remain in Russia. Listen and watch, but say little. There are troubled times ahead, perhaps dangerous for those foolish enough to speak openly what is in their minds.'

What exactly did he mean by that, Emma wondered, conscious of the sudden hardening of his expression. The look vanished as quickly as it had appeared, leaving her to wonder at the momentary flicker of fear it had instilled in her. For an instant it had been like looking at a total stranger.

Was she being reminded she was not only Maritza's companion, but her watch-dog too, answerable to him for her every movement? Or was there a deeper, more alarming insinuation which referred to the growing conflict between the Czar Peter and his estranged wife? In such a marital situation it was inevitable friends and colleagues would take opposing sides. How dangerous was it to be, as he was, a close confidant of Catherine? How unwise not to be a friend of the unstable Peter, or to openly voice dissatisfaction with his rule, as she had heard several people do today?

'Have you made your peace with Anne?'

Emma shook her head. She realised she should by now have gone to her cousin and attempted to heal the rift between them.

'Not yet.'

'Then you must do so now. I do not want the bad feeling between you to continue. She must accept the fact you are to stay, and accept it gracefully. She is coming this way. Let us settle the matter once and for all.'

Emma did not have a chance to protest. As Anne and Nikolai approached, Michael stepped forward and kissed his new sister-in-law on both cheeks.

'You look radiant, my dear. I was just telling Emma you are being admired by every woman in the room. And you, my brother, are the envy of every man. But I think you know that already.'

Michael clasped Nikolai's hand in a firm grip. Emma wondered if anyone else realised how close the bond between them really was, an understanding which went far beyond the blood ties which bound them together. She had sensed it often, especially when Nikolai had spoken of his elder brother. As for Michael, the pride in his eyes as he stepped back to her side proclaimed the depths of his own feelings.

What kind of woman would Michael choose for himself, Emma wondered? He had said he would marry within a year, but even his own sister confessed she knew nothing of the bride he had selected.

What woman in the whole of Russia could step into the shoes of the Czarina Catherine—was rich enough to bestow favours on him such as he must enjoy under her patronage?

Michael's gaze was on her as he waited for her to make the first move.

'May I be allowed to congratulate you both? Anne, I hope you will be very happy.' Her cousin did not move, her face was frozen into a mask of open displeasure. Emma kissed her briefly on one cheek before she deliberately turned away. 'Prince Nikolai . . .' The hand she extended towards Nikolai was accepted with a warm smile. As if to compensate for his wife's rudeness, he lifted it to his lips and laid a gentle kiss on her fingertips.

'I am very pleased you have graced us with your presence, little cousin. Maritza tells me you will be staying for a few more days.'

'Emma has agreed to remain as our sister's companion,' Michael broke in as Anne turned to glare daggers at her cousin. 'It is time I allowed Maritza more freedom. Under the watchful eye of one so capable I shall have no fear of her running off with the first handsome rogue who takes her fancy.' His light tone gave no indication of the concern he had previously shown when acquainting Emma of his sister's undesirable entanglement and his intentions of curtailing it at all costs.

Musicians seated in the long gallery above the ballroom struck up a minuet and immediately the conversation dwindled and died away and all eyes turned in the direction of the newly-weds.

The transformation in Anne was instantaneous. Smiling, she laid a ringed hand on Nikolai's arm, said in a honey-sweet tone:

'Everyone is waiting for us to open the dancing.'

Emma caught her breath at the thoughtless remark. She knew full well that Nikolai, with his disability, never went near a dance floor.

'Damn you,' he said in a low, fierce whisper. Emma thought if he could have got his hands near Anne's throat he would have throttled her. This was the woman he loved, yet who, even on their wedding day, could not resist the temptation to humiliate him. Emma's heart went out to him and then her pity turned to anger as Anne said pointedly:

'Michael, if Nikolai refuses to partner me, then you must. Everyone is waiting. I am being shamed before all these people because my husband is not man enough to overcome his disability, even for the sake of his pride.'

'You will soon discover Nikolai is more than man enough for you, my dear Anne,' Michael replied, his mouth deepening into a humourless smile; but to Emma's utter disgust, he offered his arm and led her into the middle of the floor.

The surprised buzz of conversation which sprang up lasted only a brief moment before they were joined on the floor by other dancers, but the curious, often sympathetic, sometimes speculative glances cast in Nikolai's direction, continued throughout the evening.

As Anne was partnered time and time again by different men, but never her husband, Emma sensed his frustration building to a dangerous level. She tried to hold him in conversation, but after a while he shut his ears to her chatter and turned all his attention to the large glasses of vodka he was drinking.

Sick at heart Emma could watch the spectacle no longer, and hurried from the room. Anne had degraded her husband in public. She had only herself to blame for any repercussions which might arise, and something told her that Nikolai was not the kind of man, despite his disability, to ignore the pointed insult.

As she passed the library on her way towards the stairs she heard the shrill tones of a woman's voice raised in anger and then the distinct sound of a slap. The next moment the door was flung open and a tearful young maid came running out, holding a hand against a smarting cheek. In the room beyond Emma saw a woman, shrouded in furs, standing before a blazing fire. She was shaking snow from her dark hair and shivering violently. A late guest, was Emma's immediate thought, probably caught in a snow-drift which Michael had hinted could possibly block the roads to the Adashev estates at this time of year.

Hesitantly she stepped nearer. Large expressive blue eyes swept her from head to toe with a haughty stare which almost made her turn and leave, but as the woman began to shiver again, she hurried forward.

'You look frozen. Let me help you off with your coat. Can I fetch you something warm to drink? Some mulled wine perhaps?'

Snowflakes showered the floor as she removed the sumptuous fur cloak and laid it across a nearby chair.

'A large glass of Michael's excellent port might do the trick.' When Emma looked about her, at a loss as to where to find the decanters, a slender sapphire-ringed hand was waved in the direction of the lower half of an enormous oak bookcase. This woman was no stranger to the house, she realised.

She was strikingly beautiful, her flawless skin set off to perfection against thick hair adorned with pearls. Her gown was midnight-blue velvet, the bodice slashed with white satin ribbons and the skirt divided to reveal several tiers of white Brussels lace. Emma gave a gasp of dismay as she caught sight of a large tear several inches above the hem.

'That's why I slapped the idiot girl who brought me in here,' the woman said with an annoyed frown. 'Clumsy little fool! I had this made especially for Prince Nikolai's wedding and now it is ruined.'

'May I?' Emma said and went down on one knee, lifting the damaged velvet onto the palm of her hand. 'It could be repaired.' Ruined indeed! A few hours work and she could have it as good as new.

She rose quickly to her feet as the door opened and Michael Adashev entered and closed it securely behind him. Emma's eyes widened in astonishment as he crossed the room to where the woman stood, took both her hands in his and raised them to his lips. Emma might not have existed.

'What an appalling journey you must have had. My steward tells me it has taken four hours,' he said. Was it relief, or pleasure, she heard in his voice?

'And I intend to spend the next four before a roaring fire enjoying the best your cellars can offer me, Michael. I hope you will join me. We have much to discuss.'

'No-one told me you were here . . .'

'I slipped in the back way. Too many curious eyes out front. The wedding went well?'

'The bride has just retired.'

'A pity. I wanted to see for myself this red-headed beauty you chose. No matter, tomorrow will do, although I cannot stay as long as I first thought. If my apartments are ready I will go upstairs directly. Come to me in an hour when I am in a better humour.'

Emma was beginning to have more than just a suspicion as to the identity of the stranger as Michael released her and stepped back. His companion added:

'This young woman has been very kind. She provided me with fortification against the cold.'

'This is the other English girl I spoke of,' Michael answered. 'Your Imperial Majesty, may I present Emma Fraser.'

Catherine gave an amused laugh as Emma sank into a deep curtsey. The Czarina herself, and she had been talking to her, offering advice as if . . . Her tongue would be the death of her one day.

'You have embarrassed the poor child, Michael. She was about to tell me what a simple task it will be to repair my ruined gown and I think I shall give her the chance to show me what she can do. I should welcome a dressmaker with fresh ideas.'

'I am sure Your Majesty will have no cause to be displeased with my work,' Emma murmured.

'We shall see.'

Michael summoned a servant who showed no surprise at the woman he was to escort upstairs. He had obviously been well briefed beforehand, Emma thought, and it confirmed her suspicions that Catherine was no stranger to the house.

She watched the regal figure gracefully climb the marble staircase, followed by a bevy of personal attendants and several trunks.

She had met the most famous woman in Russia! She sensed a strong personality behind those beautiful features. Strong enough—perhaps determined enough—to be involved in plots to remove her husband from the throne, as recent rumours had suggested. One thing was certain, she had the beauty to attact, and to bind men to her, powerful landowners, high-ranking officers, princes of the realm, like the man at her side.

She stole a glance into his face. His gaze followed Catherine until she disappeared from sight. In an hour he would be with her . . .

'Anne will be so pleased the Czarina has arrived after

all,' she murmured and his expression betrayed instant disapproval.

'She will be told in the morning. Do not bother her now.'

'It is no bother . . .'

He interrupted her with a fierce expletive.

'Have I not made myself clear? Maritza is now your concern, not Anne. I suggest you return to your duties and leave your cousin in the capable hands of her husband.'

'Indeed.' Emma's tone grew cool as she stared into the ballroom where Nikolai was laughing with a group of men. He was swaying unsteadily and, even as she watched, plucked yet another full glass of wine from the tray of a hovering servant.

'Prince Nikolai will be capable of falling asleep and that is all,' she returned.

'No Adashev yet to my knowledge has failed to fulfil his marital duties,' Michael answered bitingly. 'Please return to Maritza and remain with her until she retires.'

He spun on his heel and strode towards the staircase. Emma turned blindly back into the room, fighting back a rush of tears as she stood in the doorway. She could see no sign of Maritza.

Nikolai caught sight of her, left his companions and limped to her side.

'You look lost, little cousin.'

'I am looking for your sister.'

'Out on the terrace, suitably chaperoned by an aged aunt. Why are you sad, little Emma?' A gentle hand was laid on her arm. He had consumed enough drink this evening to make him drunk, Emma thought, but as she looked into his eyes she was sure he was in control of every one of his faculties. Was it an act for the benefit of his friends? If so, why? Again she was made to remember the brief moments they had shared when he had smashed a glass and cut himself and she had bandaged the injury. He had been drinking then, but he had been sober the moment his brother arrived. He was play-acting! Anne had accused him of not being a whole man—not only a cripple, but a drunkard. He could do nothing to straighten his leg and so he was using his drinking as a weapon against her.

'Tell her you love her. Make her believe you,' Emma pleaded. 'For your sake as well as hers. You could be happy . . .'

'How naïve you are,' Nikolai said, not unkindly. 'She needs time. We both do. Michael would not have brought her to Russia if he had not been sure of her.'

Michael—always Michael! Was he to overshadow forever the lives of everyone, including herself? Emma forced a smile to her stiff lips, but could find no words to answer him.

As Nikolai reached the top of the stairs, Michael appeared and called to him, but she could not hear what he said, for the sound of laughter behind her drowned the words. The two men moved out of sight, with Michael's arm carelessly wrapped around his brother's shoulders. One man was going to his wife . . . the other . . .

CHAPTER FIVE

It was four o'clock in the morning before Emma eventually climbed wearily into bed after leaving Maritza safely in her room. She slept soundly until ten, and then, when she awoke, found a young girl quietly picking up the clothes she had discarded. She had not bothered to put anything away. The yellow dress, her petticoats and shift were lying across the chaise-longue, her shoes lay in the middle of the carpet. She had wanted only to sleep, to rid her mind of the image of Michael closeted together with Catherine.

'Mademoiselle is ready for her breakfast?' Emma drew herself up, only half awake and stared at her questioningly. 'I am Annushka. I am yours to command.'

Emma blinked at her unbelievingly. A maid of her very own! Her new position had brought with it more advantages than she had anticipated.

'Breakfast? Yes, thank you. Is anyone up yet—Princess Maritza, or my cousin.' She almost said Anne, but corrected herself in time, 'the Princess Adasheva?'

'It is only a little after ten,' Annushka replied in a surprised tone. 'No-one will be up before noon, except the seigneur . . . he always rises at six.'

The seigneur—the elder. She meant Michael.

'Very well, Annushka, you may bring me something to eat.'

She slid out of bed, splashed some cold water into a bowl and laid a wet towel across her throbbing temples. How her head ached this morning, but she had only taken two glasses of champagne, so she knew that was not the cause.

Maritza had danced her partners into the ground, and

Emma herself had been so much in demand that she had not lacked a companion for the remainder of the evening. Yet she had been unable to enjoy herself. She could dismiss the truth no longer. She was falling in love with Michael Adashev! So much for her resolve never to allow herself to become emotionally involved with any man! She was too much like her beloved mother. She would love and love deeply—loyally—only one man until the end of her days. The knowledge brought with it little comfort.

The Czarina's damaged gown was brought while Emma was brushing her hair. She studied the rent, prayed she had been correct in her assumption she could mend it without any problem, and set about the task immediately.

Emma's composure was completely shattered when the door was suddenly flung open and Anne came running into the room, her eyes red and swollen from crying. At the sight of her cousin calmly sewing, she burst into another flood of wild tears. All antagonism was forgotten as Emma threw aside her work to try and comfort the distraught girl.

'Anne, what is it?'

'I hate him,' Anne wailed, between sobs. 'I hate him, do you hear?'

'Nikolai? Why, what has he done?' Emma asked, aghast.

'No, not Nikolai,' her cousin sniffled. 'Michael—he is cruel—a monster.'

'Sit down and tell me all about it.' Emma's attempts to calm her were in vain. Anne paced the floor like a caged animal, clenching and unclenching her fists, and as the tears slowly began to subside, hatred burned in her eyes.

'Do you know what I have just been told? We are not to live here at Malayevka. This is Michael's house. As the elder brother he inherited everything on the death of his father. Nikolai has nothing but a desolate house three miles away and an income which Michael provides. Michael owns everything.'

'Does that really matter?' Emma asked quietly. 'It will give you and Nikolai a chance to get to know each other away from Michael's influence. I think it will be a good thing.'

'How dare you presume to tell me what is good for me. We shall be marooned there—without friends.'

'It is only three miles away,' Emma insisted, but her cousin was beyond reason. She stared at Emma through narrowed eyes and the look in them was not pleasant. Slowly she turned and looked around the room, as comfortably furnished as her own, and her pallor grew.

'You don't care, do you? Why should you. You think he finds you attractive, don't you? Well, you are wrong.'

'I don't know what you mean,' Emma replied, stiffening.

'Just because he was nice to you once, do you think that means anything to a man like him?' She gave a brittle laugh as Emma's cheeks began to burn with embarrassment. 'If only you could have seen yourself yesterday—parading around like—like a kept woman! Irene told me where the dress had come from and we both know who told Maritza to be so generous, don't we? Mama always said you were a sly little minx—just like your mother.'

Emma choked back the bitter words which rose to her lips, somehow restrained the urge to lash out at the lovely face twisted with malice. That would only bring her down to Anne's level.

'May we come in?'

Michael and Maritza stood in the open doorway. Emma wished the floor would open up and swallow her. She needed only one glance into their faces to see they had overheard Anne's spiteful remarks. Poor Maritza looked near to tears, and Michael . . . The smile on his face did not match the smouldering anger in the depths of his pale eyes.

'Maritza has offered to help you finish your packing, Anne. The carriage will be ready within the hour,' he said in a pleasant tone.

'Of course—there is so much to take with you,' Maritza said. She flashed a smile in Emma's direction. 'I came to tell you how pleased I am you have decided to stay.'

Her lips compressed into a tight line, Anne brushed past them both, almost knocking Maritza over in the process, making it painfully clear of her opposition to the elevation of her cousin in the household.

'Oh, dear, I think I have said the wrong thing again,' Maritza declared and, picking up her skirts, ran out of the room after her.

'Maritza is usually such a quiet child, there are times when I forget she has inherited our father's strength of character and has a tendency to speak her own mind,' Michael murmured, stepping across to the chair where Catherine's gown lay. His fingers lightly touched the blue velvet and then, as if the sight of it disturbed him, he moved to the window and stood watching the snow drift past outside.

'I would hardly describe the Princess as a child,' Emma ventured to answer. 'She is a young woman.'

'Meaning?' He quirked an eyebrow at her questioningly.

'Her world here seems so—confined. She needs the company of people her own age. She must be allowed to spread her wings a little or I am afraid that, pushed too far in the wrong direction, she might rebel against your authority.'

'And elope with the man of her choice despite my opposition? She won't though, will she, because you are here to look after her as efficiently as you cared for your cousin. Do not think your task is going to be an easy one. Maritza can be as wilful and rebellious as a dozen Annes put together.'

'Then does she not need a friend and not a watchdog?'

'By all means be her friend, but never allow that friendship to conflict with your first duty, your loyalty to me. In the final analysis I shall be the judge of what is best for her,' Michael answered in a cool tone.

'As you have decided what is best for Anne, whether she wishes it or not. Could you not have been a little more gentle, more understanding than to have packed her off the day after her wedding?'

'How am I in the wrong there? She has a fine house and servants and a husband who adores her, despite her failings. The marriage will succeed if they are left alone. You have been her crutch for far too long. She must now learn to stand on her own two feet and to turn to Nikolai, not to you.'

'You place too much importance on our relationship,' Emma protested.

'Your cousin is a beautiful, calculating young woman who will put her new position to good use, and use others as she has used you in the past. In a few days she will have forgotten you exist.'

Emma could not deny the truth of his words. She had always been used, and she knew it, but that did not stop his words from hurting.

'You are satisfied with your accommodation?' He changed the subject so abruptly that Emma was momentarily taken aback.

'Yes, thank you,' she stammered at last.

'And the girl Annushka? She was only purchased a week ago, but she seems willing enough, and I have had good reports about her.'

'I did not expect . . .' Emma's voice trailed off into a horrified silence. 'Did you say she had been bought? Like—like a slave? That is terrible! Surely she is no more than fourteen. Where are her parents?'

'I have no idea of her age and I'm sure she could not tell us who her mother and father were,' Michael replied, and the indifference in his tone shocked her still further. Folding his arms he leaned back against the wall and the casual pose served to irritate her further. He was so sure of himself, of everyone! What did he care for the poor wretches who tilled his fields, cared for his animals, waited on him hand and foot, every minute of the day

. . . made him rich from the sweat of their brow?

'I find it quite unbelievable that one person should go through life being owned body and soul by another human being.' She forced the words out, forgetful at that moment how her own life, until a very short time ago, had been on a comparable level with his serfs. She had never been beaten or starved, but she had owned nothing and had depended solely on the charity of others for food and a roof over her head.

'Come now,' Michael said, still apparently unperturbed by her show of antagonism. 'Do not compare us to those who traffic in the slave-trade—and I speak of your own countrymen. Did English judges not exile thousands of Scots men and women to a life of bondage in the New World after the failing of Charles Stuart to seize the throne in 1745? Indentured servants they were called, but it was slavery of a bestial nature, and few ever survived to earn their freedom.'

'You are quite correct, sir,' Emma said, rather annoyed at his knowledge of her own country. Had her father survived Culloden he would have been among those poor unfortunate wretches sentenced to deportation to Virginia or some other god-forsaken outback. 'England does not have an unblemished record, and I dislike the things that have happened there as intensely as I disapprove of the barbarism I find in this country.'

'So you would abolish serfdom. What would they do then? Most of the servants in this house were born on the estate, like their fathers and grandfathers before them. This is their home.'

'What choice have they?' Emma challenged, and the gleam which entered his eyes warned her that his patience was at an end.

'I have found our conversation most exhilarating, mademoiselle, but I shall have to leave your questions unanswered for now. Your cousin will be departing soon. I suggest you say your farewells downstairs and so avoid a repetition of the rather emotional scene I witnessed earlier.'

'As you wish,' Emma murmured, her tone now demure.

As Michael reached the door, he paused and looked back at her, and his final words warned her the scathing comments she had flung at him were neither to be overlooked, nor forgiven.

'You are a worthy adversary, my little English miss, but the next time we cross swords, you will not achieve such an easy victory.'

Nikolai and Anne, the latter enveloped from head to toe in a magnificent white ermine cloak, a wedding present from the Czarina Catherine, were in the drawing-room when Emma went downstairs. Like Michael, she did not want another scene and was relieved to find that her cousin had composed herself sufficiently to say goodbye in a manner that was not unfriendly. Nikolai's doing—or had Michael been talking to her, painting an idyllic scene of life at Belmaya? Her assumption seemed to be correct, for Nikolai turned to her with a smile and said.

'In a few weeks, when Anne has had a chance to organise everything to her satisfaction, we shall hold a ball. You will come, of course.'

'I would like that very much.'

'And Maritza is coming over next week to take tea with us. You will accompany her, of course,' Anne added. It sounded more like an order than an invitation, but Emma nodded.

'Please send word when it is convenient. I will write to Lord and Lady Tarrant at once and inform them how well everything went, and that you will be writing to them yourself when you have a spare moment.' Emma saw Michael frown slightly at the suggestion, but could find no reason why he should object. Anne's parents would be desperate for news by now. She would send her letter, with or without his permission.

Anne pecked at Emma's cheek, embraced Maritza, and then Irene followed her mistress out to the carriage, to tuck still more furs over her and slip stone hot-water bottles between the rugs draped over her feet. Emma left Nikolai talking to his brother and sister and returned to the house.

Seated on the floor before the stove in her room, Catherine's dress spread out about her, Emma continued the delicate repair work which, when it was finished, came up to her expectations. Annushka, who had lingered to watch, was full of praise for the skill she had witnessed and seemed so eager to learn that Emma promised to teach her.

When Emma knocked at the door of the Czarina's apartment a lady in waiting opened it the slightest fraction of an inch and stared at Emma. In the room beyond, Emma could hear the sound of laughter.

'Go away—Her Imperial Majesty cannot be disturbed,' she hissed.

'Who is it, Lydia?'

'Some servant girl with one of your gowns, madame. The one you damaged the other evening.'

Emma heard the sound of a man's voice and the next moment the door was swung open and she was waved inside.

Catherine, in a satin pelisse, trimmed with sable fur, lounged casually on a couch. A few feet away Michael Adashev, looking no less at ease, was seated in a high-backed chair before the fire, a decanter of wine and a glass on the ebony table beside him.

'Emma, isn't it? Come here and show me your handiwork. I am anxious to see if you are as good as I have been led to believe,' Catherine ordered, beckoning her forward.

Emma ignored the figure in the chair. He had changed into more casual attire since she had last seen him. One highly polished boot crossed over the other, he helped himself to more wine as she approached the couch and spread out the skirt of the gown for Catherine to inspect her work. What more proof did she need of his relationship with the Czarina than to find him with her at this time of day, looking for all the world as if he belonged by her side.

'She has excelled herself, as you said she would, Michael. Yet another wager lost, but well worth it this time.' Catherine's fingers examined every detail of the repair. 'Excellent—quite the best needlework I have seen. I am told you are to remain in the Adashev household. That pleases me. Bring her to Mon Plaisir the next time you come, Michael . . . and do not make me wait too long.'

'Have I ever kept your Highness waiting,' came the soft, mocking reply, and Catherine looked sideways at him with an amused laugh.

'I am pleased that your Imperial Majesty has found my work satisfactory.' The words almost stuck in Emma's throat.

'More than just satisfactory. Take this as payment for the small service you have already rendered.'

Emma stared at the ruby ring Catherine tugged from her finger and held out towards her. Payment! She had asked for none—expected none in return for the favour.

'Take it,' Michael murmured behind her and she rounded on him, her face pale and set. Had he not yet realised what she lacked in wealth she made up for in pride?

'The reward is too great for such a small task,' she said flatly. 'I am satisfied to have been of service and hope to be offered the chance to be so again in the future.'

'The girl has spirit—I like her.' Catherine sprang to her feet, gathered up the blue velvet and pressed it into Emma's arms. 'Take it, it is yours.'

Emma dared not refuse a second time.

Her last sight of Catherine was of her relaxing back on to the couch, stretching languidly. The pelisse fell open, and Emma's mind suddenly reeled with the shock of what she saw. Catherine Alexeevna, estranged wife of the Czar, was pregnant! Which one of her lovers was responsible this time? she wondered as she turned and stumbled blindly along the corridors. In her heart, she knew she did not want to know the answer . . .

Life at Malayevka was very pleasant, but quiet, Emma discovered as the days slipped by into weeks. The excitement of Christmas was over, and bad weather kept visitors away throughout the whole of January. Maritza daily grew more bored with her monotonous everyday routine, especially as the one love of her life, to ride, was impossible under the conditions which prevailed.

On the two occasions they visited Nikolai and Anne at Belmaya, despite the snow, they were shown great hospitality and friendliness, especially on the part of the former, but after they had left, Emma suspected both afternoons had been carefully planned charades. All the signs pointed to Anne settling down in her new life and enjoying it, yet Emma sensed otherwise, without one wrong word or look to confirm her suspicions.

As February arrived and the first flowers began to push their way determinedly through the still frozen ground, word arrived that the Czarina intended moving her court to the Summer Palace at Peterhof the following month, heralding a lessening of the strict mourning period she had observed since Elizabeth's death, mourning that had been rigorously enforced despite her husband's lewd comments, often voiced in public, and the total lack of respect shown for his dead aunt.

The change in Maritza was instantaneous. She began to select the clothes she would be taking with her to St Petersburg, even though Michael did not give a definite date for their departure.

That same week invitations arrived from Anne and Nikolai announcing the grande bal masqué to be held at Belmaya the following week.

One evening at dinner when Maritza allowed him to break into her excited chatter, Michael asked:

'When do you have your next fitting with Madame Thérèse?'

'Tomorrow. Wait until you see the gown I am to wear

to Belmaya, Michael. It is the most beautiful I have ever owned. Emma chose the material for me and made some alterations to Madame Thérèse's design. You will not recognise me when I am masked.'

Emma saw Michael's eyes narrow fractionally as if the thought disturbed him. The bal masqué would be a perfect opportunity for Maritza to flirt with her beau, if he had been invited, or with any handsome young man who took her fancy. And she was just wilful enough to do it and pay her brother back for the long months of seclusion he had forced her to endure.

'I am sure you will dazzle everyone, as usual. While Madame Thérèse is with you, I think it a good idea she should begin preparing a wardrobe for Mademoiselle Fraser, don't you?'

'I have adequate clothes for my present needs,' Emma broke in, paling slightly.

'We both know that is untrue,' Michael replied coolly. 'You forget I am soon to take you to Mon Plaisir. Catherine will have my blood if you appear before her in rags. I expect you to take your responsibilities seriously and dress as now befits your position in my household. I hope I make myself quite clear.'

When he put it that way she had little choice, Emma thought.

Michael tapped a ringed finger against the side of the silver goblet in front of him in an impatient gesture, as he awaited an answer.

'As you wish,' Emma murmured and caught the flash of surprise which crossed his face.

So Catherine still wanted to see her! She had not taken the suggestion seriously, especially as it had not been mentioned since. She would certainly need a new dress for that occasion, and travelling clothes too!

She became aware of Michael watching her and the smile which deepened the corners of his mouth caused a brief moment of irritation. No doubt he was waiting for her to take full advantage of his generous offer, as Anne would have done, making her as beholden to him as any other member of his household. How he loved to remind her of his absolute power over everyone, the servants, his own sister—everyone except herself. Her chin tilting determinedly, expecting opposition, she said:

'I must insist on paying for my own clothes.'

'It has always been the custom for the Master of Malayevka to feed and clothe those he employs, but if it will appease that stubborn English pride, then I will deduct a little from your salary each month. Does that satisfy you?'

'Perfectly. Thank you.'

Immediately he changed the subject and informed them that the house in St Petersburg would be ready to receive them at the beginning of May. If he was expecting the news to bring gladness, he was mistaken. Maritza had clearly expected it to be much sooner.

'Oh, no, Michael, that is unbearable,' she declared. 'Have you no heart? I miss my friends . . . Julia and the Princess Myagky and Paula Petrinsky . . .'

'And Vasily Zouroff?' He tossed the name at her, his tone changing.

Instantly Emma knew this was the man of whom he disapproved. Maritza sat bolt upright in her chair. There was not only defiance in her young face, but something Emma had never seen before—resentment.

'I have done all you asked of me. I have not written, nor received a letter from him since you brought me back to Malayevka last August.'

August! Six months since she had been in the company of people her own age, friends with whom she could confide, Emma thought sympathetically. Apart from the occasional visitor she had been totally isolated, and deliberately. How could Michael, who she was sure loved his sister deeply, be so insensitive to the needs of a young girl fast growing into a desirable young woman?

Anne had been in love, or so she called it, many times—and out of it more times than Emma could remember. Laughter, tears, accusations, recriminations, Emma had suffered them all, as had the unfortunate parents. Now Emma was more aware of the Tarrant's circumstances, she could fully understand the dilemma they had been in. Anne had high ambitions. Nothing less than a lord or duke for her, and there was no way her parents could find the dowry required for such a match.

Michael had worked so hard to make his brother happy, yet he turned his back on his sister, who needed not only his love and protection, but his understanding. Most of all that!

Tears trembled in Maritza's eyes. For a moment Emma thought she meant to force the issue into the open. Then with immense dignity she excused herself and left the room. Emma also rose to her feet, unable to bring herself to remain in Michael's presence one moment longer. As she pushed back her chair he looked up at her, his face an expressionless mask.

'When you know the full facts, then judge me,' he said.

'Is your conscience not judging you now, sir.' She flung the words back at him without thinking.

Michael's fingers tightened around the goblet he held until the knuckles grew white. For a brief instant she thought he meant to throw it at her, and she took an involuntary step backwards.

'My sister will have need of you,' came the terse reply.

As she closed the door behind her, Emma looked back. Jan was pouring more wine into his empty goblet and she watched him drain it without appreciation. He looked so alone! It was the first time she had ever considered that Michael Adashev, despite his title and lands, the wealth and position he commanded, the favours of the first lady in the land—might possibly be a lonely man.

Maritza's mood had not improved when she came unexpectedly to Emma's room the following afternoon. She was still bitter and resentful of the fact she was to be kept at Malayevka for another six weeks. It showed in her pale face as she threw herself down into a chair and ordered Annushka to fetch tea for them both.

Emma had never known her to be so sullen and uncommunicative before. Michael had a fight on his hands, she realised. He would, must, win in the end, but in doing so it was possible he might lose not only the respect but also the love of his sister. Could this Vasily Zouroff mean so much to her she would risk everything to be with him, even Michael's wrath and possible disinheritance if all other methods failed?

With a soft sigh Emma began to gather up the dresses she had earlier draped over the bed. She still could not make up her mind what to wear to the bal masqué.

'I like the blue,' Maritza declared sitting upright. 'Isn't that the one the Czarina gave you?'

'Yes. It's lovely, isn't it? But—but dare I wear it—it is so grand?' Emma held it against her. She had shortened the skirt and taken in the bodice to fit her own modest bosom. Maritza's eyes gleamed with a sudden mischievous look.

'You will be masked—who will know who you are? Think of all the men who will pursue you thinking you are some rich titled lady from St Petersburg or Moscow.' Emma did not care for the cynical note which crept into her tone.

'Surely you are not going to be intimidated by what my brother might think?' Maritza added, sensing Emma's indecision.

Slowly Emma laid the dress aside, the colour ebbing from her cheeks. It was not like Maritza to be so sarcastic. Michael had hurt her more deeply than he realised.

'I'm sorry.' Maritza sprang from her chair and hugged her, suddenly contrite. 'I am little more than a prisoner in this place, Emma, and it has made me forget my manners. Keeping me here all summer was Michael's way of teaching me a lesson, the beast, because I opposed his orders. He does not like to be disobeyed, especially by a frail woman, incapable of thinking for

herself. We are supposed to be so dependent on men, allowing them to make all the decisions and just look pretty when they demand it. Egotists! We have to lie in their beds and bear their children while they go off and enjoy themselves without a thought as to what we might want. Well, I want more out of my life than to be married off to the man of my brother's choice like a chattel, to find myself swollen and unsightly with child before I have even learned how to be a woman.'

'Believe me, Maritza, you are a woman,' Emma interposed softly.

Maritza stepped back, flushing at her words.

'I—I am only eighteen. Both Nikolai and Michael treat me as if I am still a child though.'

'You think like a woman—'

'Then why does Michael treat me as if I am still a babe in arms?'

'For him perhaps, the change in you is harder to accept than you realise. He is too used to taking care of you. Brothers are like that sometimes. They can be more jealous than a husband or sweetheart.' How experienced she sounded, yet she had known neither brother nor sweetheart.

'I wish that was true,' Maritza said with a sigh, dropping back into her chair, 'but I think not. He is afraid I shall disgrace the name of Adashev by marrying beneath me. He deprives me of what I want, yet applies a different set of rules to suit his own needs. He can have any woman he pleases, including the Czarina herself.'

'You are expecting him to respect the feelings you have for this Vasily Zouroff because he is flesh and blood too and does not deny himself the rights you demand for yourself. But can you not see how different the circumstances are?'

'Is he flesh and blood, I sometimes wonder? Tell me about my brother, Emma. I suspect you know him almost as well as I do,' Maritza interrupted. 'No other person has ever dared to speak to him as you do—no servant, that is. He will brook no argument once he has made a decision, yet he allows you to voice an opinion. He has had men whipped for less insolence than you show him at times. Be careful you do not provoke him too far. There is a devil in him you would not find pleasant. I saw him angry once, when I was a little girl. I have never forgotten it. I wonder if any other woman has ever seen him that way?'

'Are you referring to any woman in particular, little sister?' Michael drawled from the doorway.

Maritza gave a startled gasp and bright colour stained her cheeks as he advanced into the room. She was terrified he might have overheard earlier parts of the conversation, Emma realised. He was dressed to go out and carried a fur coat over one arm.

'Where are you going?' Maritza asked. Her voice trembled slightly, but she was rapidly regaining her composure. 'Sit down and take tea with us, I have hardly seen you all day.'

'My horse is saddled and I shall be late for an appointment if I stay. But I can spare a moment.' Michael lowered himself into a chair. 'I shall be at Peterhof until the end of the week. If you behave yourself I might be persuaded to bring you back a present.'

'A large bottle of French perfume to overwhelm Anne's guests at the bal masqué,' Maritza returned. 'You will be back in time?'

'Naturally. What are these?' Michael leaned forward and picked up several pieces of paper which were lying on a nearby table. 'These are very good. Who did them?'

'I did,' Emma said, wishing he had not seen them. She had shown them to no-one, not even Maritza. They were a very personal part of her; together they made up the wardrobe she would someday own. She had spent hours on each one, perfecting them in every detail and now Michael, of all people, was scrutinising each one in turn.

'Yet another talent you seem reluctant to reveal,' he murmured. 'You have not answered my question, Maritza. What woman?'

Fully in control of herself once again, Maritza

bestowed on him a disarming smile.

'I was debating which one of your many lady friends you will be escorting to the bal masqué,' she replied.

'With two attractive young women already at my side I think that will be sufficient,' Michael answered good-humouredly. As he rose to his feet the sketches still in one hand, he added: 'I would like to show these to the Czarina if you have no objections, mademoiselle?'

'None at all.' How could she refuse? He was already tucking them inside his coat.

Maritza ran to the window to watch him ride off, together with Jan close behind, but the smile disappeared from her face as she turned back into the room.

'He will only be away a few days,' Emma said consolingly.

'He is going to Catherine, you know that, don't you?' She sounded disturbed.

'It is none of my concern.'

'Or mine either. But, really, it is, Emma. Oh, I know we disagree over Vasily, but I have learned my lesson there. When we return to St Petersburg I will see him as often as I wish, without Michael's permission, and risk his anger. His association with Catherine is something else. He has made countless enemies because of his closeness to her, people who were once his friends. She has other men, why does she want him too? She will have destroyed him if the Czar ever succeeds in being rid of her . . . without her, anything could happen to Michael. Imprisonment—banishment—a knife in the back one dark night. Surely he must realise the risks?'

'Perhaps he considers them worth while,' Emma said gently.

'I wish he would marry and settle down at Malayevka with his horses. He could have the pick of at least a dozen eligible women in St Petersburg.'

So Michael had not mentioned his forthcoming marriage plans to his sister. Did he consider the event so unimportant?

CHAPTER SIX

ON the day of the bal masqué at Belmaya, Emma's maid, Annushka, disappeared. Returning to her rooms in the afternoon, after being with an excited Maritza, she found the bed unmade and clothes still lying across a chair and realised Annushka had done nothing since breakfast. Even the tray was still beside the bed. It was so unlike the maid who was usually eager to please, Emma thought.

There was no sign of her by late afternoon and Emma was forced to draw the conclusion that she had run away. She felt sad at the loss of someone she had come to consider a friend.

The flowers the girl had picked from the garden the previous day and shyly presented to her mistress looked so pretty, Emma decided to choose a few more for her sitting-room.

She was making her way back to the house when she heard the sound of a savage oath, followed by muffled groans and the heart-stopping thud of fists. She had just passed the stables where one of the grooms was unsaddling a horse, Michael's black stallion. So he had returned! The animal was lathered and breathing heavily. He had been ridden hard and mercilessly by all appearances.

'No, mademoiselle, do not go any further.'

The man stopped what he was doing to speak to her as she moved in the direction of the outhouses from where the sounds seemed to come. She turned questioningly in his direction. It sounded for all the world as if someone was being beaten.

'Why—what is happening . . . ?'

'It is not for your eyes, mademoiselle, the seigneur would not be pleased if you interfere.'

At the mention of the seigneur nothing could have stopped Emma from satisfying her curiosity. She rounded the corner and found herself behind several of the house staff. None of them saw her—all their attention was centred on the two men engaged in a fierce, bloody struggle as they rolled over and over on the ground. At least that was the way it appeared at first sight, but as she stood watching in silent horror, appalled that no-one attempted to stop the fight, she saw that one man was Michael, the other a man half his years. Each time the latter was knocked to the ground, Michael hauled him unceremoniously to his feet again by the front of a shirt which hung in ribbons and callously struck yet another blow to the bruised and battered face.

Emma pressed a hand over her mouth, choking back a cry as, with a last, brutal blow, Michael sent his opponent reeling back against the wooden shed behind him, with such violence she heard some of the panels snap under his weight.

'Get him out of my sight,' Michael snapped, and everyone ran at once, hauling the unfortunate youngster away with no more consideration than they would a dead animal. Emma was disgusted, sickened by the scene. She remembered Maritza saying how she had only ever seen her brother angry one time and then she had been afraid. Emma could understand why, as she looked across the courtyard to where he stood.

His shirt was torn and covered in blood and dirt, and blood streamed from a gash on his head. He stared after the retreating men with a look on his face which made her shudder.

She turned and ran, away from the sight of a human being hauled away like an unwanted carcass, away from the tall figure standing alone in the yard, who was suddenly a frightening stranger to her. Not until she reached her room did she stop to pause for breath.

She had been sitting in a chair for over an hour before

she became aware how dark it was outside. Annushka had not appeared to light the candles, but the girl's absence now took second place to the scene still vivid in her mind. The bal masqué had lost its attraction. Had there been some way to avoid it, she would have seized on it thankfully. Katya appeared as she was struggling to fasten the hooks of her gown to tell her Maritza was already on her way downstairs. Emma grimaced at her reflection in the glass and pinched her cheeks to bring some colour into them. Her long black hair was loose about her shoulders, held back by tortoiseshell combs. She had brushed it until it gleamed, one hundred fierce strokes of the brush and with each one she had told herself how much she hated Michael Adashev.

'A glass of wine to warm us before the journey, I think,' she heard Michael say as she reached the door of the drawing-room and steeled herself to face him as she stepped inside.

Maritza was seated in a chair, the skirts of her gown spread around her like a shower of pink apple blossom which had just fallen from the trees. A necklace of fire opals glowed at her throat. Her cheeks were flushed with excitement. Emma could see she could scarcely contain her impatience as her brother returned to her side with a drink. Beneath a long black, furlined cloak he wore rich burgundy velvet. Emma's heart lurched unsteadily as he turned in her direction with a disarming smile, but then, as she saw the vivid bruise on one cheek, the painful-looking cut just visible beneath his hairline, she was reminded of the cruelty which lay behind the smile, the savage temper which only hours before had been responsible for beating a man half to death.

'Will you take wine with us before we leave, mademoiselle?' he asked. His eyes appraised her appearance, lingering for a long moment on the hair cascading past her bare shoulders.

'Thank you, no.' Her voice betrayed the tumult raging inside her and she watched his brows draw together in a puzzled frown.

Maritza was far too engrossed in thinking about the ball to notice anything amiss. He took three unhurried strides across the room to where Emma stood, clutching her cloak and gloves and held out his own glass to her.

'The night air is still cold, and you look pale tonight. A touch of nerves perhaps?'

Nerves? Yes, but how could his nearness affect her so after what she had witnessed? He did not miss the tremor which shook the hand accepting the glass.

'I hope you will relax and enjoy yourself this evening,' his low tone did not reach the ears of his sister. 'When we return to St Petersburg, I am afraid Maritza will be so inundated with invitations you will find yourself going out every single night for a while. You may even long, as I do after only a few short weeks, to be back here at Malayevka.'

'I think I shall be—happier in St Petersburg,' Emma said. She sipped her drink and then put it aside.

'I was under the impression you liked it here . . .' Michael began and then shrugged his shoulders. 'No doubt you have your reasons for wishing to leave, personal reasons like the one which made you shiver the very first day you set foot here.'

'That was for a far different reason.' How far away that day seemed when she had stood on the steps before the house and remembered Culloden Moor.

'How so?' he demanded. 'What has happened since you have been here, since your cousin's marriage, to make you unhappy?'

'You—you ask that? After this afternoon?' The words tumbled out before she could contain them.

'What do you know of this afternoon?' Michael's tone was suddenly like a whiplash and Maritza glanced at them curiously. 'Who have you spoken to?'

'No-one . . . I saw for myself the terrible thing you did. It was monstrous, despicable. You could have killed him.' In her anger and confusion she forgot she was talking not only to a prince of royal blood, but to her employer. Had he dismissed her on the spot she would not have cared. Someone had to tell him how wrong he had been. The smile faded from his face and the eyes which searched her own were bleak and without pity.

'And who do you think you are to sit in judgment of my actions, yet again?' he demanded fiercely.

'Nothing could have justified such a show of brutality,' she flung back, and his mouth twisted sardonically.

'I used my fists when I should have used a whip,' came the chilling reply.

'On someone half your age and size. How proud that must have made you feel.' Emma was stunned by his total lack of remorse. Did he not care at all for the feelings of others?

Michael's eyes blazed blue fire, straight from the depths of hell, Emma thought weakly as she gazed into them. Nikolai had looked something like that when Anne had humiliated him in front of the wedding guests, but not so dangerous. Maritza rose to her feet declaring it was seven o'clock and they should be on their way. Michael stepped back and the relief which flooded over her left her legs feeling like water.

'When you next speak to me, mademoiselle Fraser . . .' Now she knew the extent of his displeasure. He never referred to her so formally unless she had in some way upset him '. . . it will be to apologise for those words. I suggest you ascertain the facts before you leap to conclusions in the future. Your very own future might depend on it.'

What facts? He had been taking out his temper on some unfortunate serf. His lathered horse had told her he had ridden back from Mon Plaisir in some haste, probably not taking his leave of Catherine until the last possible moment, possibly regretting the ball that made it necessary for him to leave at all. At least that had been the way it had appeared. Dear God, she thought with sudden apprehension, had she been wrong?

At the end of their journey he lifted his sister out with a whispered comment and a laugh, but Emma was left to be helped out by a servant. Her insults had drawn blood and he knew well how to exact his revenge, she realised, as she followed them at a distance into the house.

She had only herself to blame for the misery she felt, she thought, stepping into the magnificent drawing-room where Anne and Nikolai waited to greet their guests. With her face masked and wearing Catherine's gown she looked and should have felt a grand lady. Instead her only instinct was to stay as far away from everyone as possible.

If Anne was unhappy she looked the exact opposite. Her white gown was encrusted with hundreds of different precious stones which shimmered in the candle-light. Around her throat she wore the solitaire diamond, and more diamonds sparkled around her wrists and in her ears. She was shaking hands with each new arrival, smiling, radiant. Emma was quite taken aback. Either her cousin had resolved her differences with her husband or she was putting on a very good act for the benefit of those around her.

'Emma! Welcome, little cousin.' Nikolai suddenly broke off his conversation and turned in her direction. Michael took Maritza by the arm and they moved on. 'With that black hair I knew you at once, despite that splendid dress.'

Behind her golden mask Anne's eyes gleamed with sudden derision as she surveyed the elegant figure before her, and Emma waited for some shattering remark to further upset the evening. To her surprise Anne leaned forward and lightly brushed her cheek with her lips.

'Maritza may find she has competition tonight, eh Nikolai? You look charming, Emma. Now run along and enjoy yourself. No, wait—you do not know anyone here. Come with me and I will introduce you to some of my friends.'

Not waiting for an answer she moved off and Emma knew she was expected to follow.

Her face wreathed in smiles, her voice all honeyed sweetness, hiding the deep resentment which lurked behind her action, Anne allowed everyone to know in no uncertain terms that the slender, attractively gowned young woman at her side was not a guest in the true sense of the word, but her cousin who had accompanied her to Russia before her marriage. Due to the unfortunate state of her circumstances she had prevailed upon Prince Michael to find her some position, feeling duty bound because of their blood ties to secure her future in some way—and he had graciously consented to engage her as companion to his sister.

Within half-an-hour there was not one person in the room who did not know who, and what, Emma was. None of the women came near her and the husbands were quickly whisked away if they attempted to engage her in conversation. Several young men danced with her and only one did not try to make an assignation with her. The kind of treatment they reserved for servant girls, Emma thought shamefaced, as she tried to lose herself in a corner.

'I think you are in need of something to put the colour back into those pale cheeks.' Nikolai was at her side with two glasses of wine. She did not refuse, and allowed him to lead her away from the throng to the quiet of the corridor. 'You are not dancing. What is wrong?'

'Nothing . . . there are so many people . . .' she said with a shaky laugh. Nikolai was so sweet, so trusting. How could she tell him the truth and perhaps provoke even more bad feeling between himself and Anne. 'I find it all rather overwhelming.'

'It is only a beginning. When we return to Petersburg the invitations will come flooding in, you'll see.'

'Prince Michael did warn me of your sister's popularity.'

'I meant for you, Emma. I have noticed the young men eyeing you ever since you came in. Come now, don't tell me you haven't noticed too.'

Michael passed close by them with an attractive brunette on his arm. Emma was conscious of his gaze narrowing as he recognised her companion. Did he still frown on her friendship with Nikolai, innocent though it was? Or did he still smart from her earlier outburst?

'I am glad to see Michael is enjoying himself. After this afternoon I thought he might not come.'

'So you know about that too,' Emma said, in a hollow tone, and he looked down into her pale face with a grave nod.

'But of course. Michael stopped here on his way to Malayevka. He often does when he has been to Peterhof. It was he who found the unfortunate girl in the woods not a mile from here. He brought her back and then led the search party himself for her attacker. I hear he thrashed the man to within an inch of his life. If it had been me I would have hung him from the nearest tree.'

'I—I'm sorry. I don't understand . . . what girl?' Emma's voice was hardly audible.

Nikolai's expression changed instantly to one of great concern.

'Devil take me for a fool! From the way you spoke I thought you knew. After he left here around noon today Michael came across the body of a girl in some bushes. She had been brutally raped and left for dead. Of course he brought her here to be attended by my own doctor, but the poor child died. Mercifully however, before she breathed her last, she managed to name the animal who had savaged her.'

'Go on, please. I must know what happened.' Emma fought down the nausea rising in her stomach.

'Very well, if you insist, but not here. Come with me.'

Nikolai took her into a side room, closed the door and pushed her gently towards the nearest chair.

'Sit down. Are you going to be all right?'

'I—I was very rude to your brother this evening . . .' the words tumbled out in a rush. 'You see, I saw him fighting . . . and . . .'

'You thought he was the kind of man to thrash another without good reason?' Nikolai returned, perching himself on the arm of a chair, opposite her.

'It looked that way at the time.' She had suspected he was in a foul mood because he had dragged himself away from the side of the Czarina, but she could not speak her thoughts aloud, knowing full well they would betray the secret she harboured.

'Never. Michael is the fairest man I know. True, he has a temper, but he can control it, believe me.'

'I used my fists when I should have used a whip.' He had given the man a chance to fight back, which is more than had been afforded the unfortunate victim.

'Why—why did he not tell me when I challenged him?'

'Challenged him!' Nikolai interrupted. 'My dear girl, that is the worst thing you could have done. Besides, under the circumstances, he did not want to cause you pain, tonight of all nights. The girl who was ravished was your maid, Annushka.'

Emma gave an inarticulate cry and the glass fell from her hand on to the floor. Everything was suddenly so horribly clear . . . she had condemned the man who had captured Annushka's attacker as a sadistic brute, without feelings, without scruples.

'He was right not to tell you. He suspected you had grown too fond of the girl despite the short time she has been with you,' Nikolai said gently. He pressed a lace handkerchief into her hand and she began to wipe the wine from the blue velvet. Her mind was numb, refusing to accept the terrible crime which had been committed.

'Only this morning I promised to give her an embroidery lesson. Dear God, this is an inhuman country! She was so young.' She fought back the impulse to burst into tears.

'No, Emma, only some of the people who live in it. Come now, you must not grieve.'

'I agree with you. I would have hanged him on the spot,' she cried. 'Why was he allowed to go free?'

'At times it is very easy to take the life of another human being. Michael has been a soldier—he knows this. They pay for their crimes in one brief moment of agony, but it is often a quicker death than these scoundrels mete out to their victims,' Nikolai returned. 'Michael chose to ensure he suffered, the way Annushka had suffered. He handed him over to the other villagers. They will ensure he will never attack another woman. He will live, but not as a whole man.'

A far more drastic fate than if he had indeed been hung on the spot, Emma realised. Gradually her composure began to return and with it the realisation that she had an apology to make to Michael.

'Emma.' Nikolai leaned towards her, suddenly grave-faced. 'Are we truly friends? I am desperately in need of advice and I have no-one to turn to. No-one who, I suspect, will be as honest with their answers as you.'

Emma thrust the unpleasant task which lay ahead of her to the back of her mind.

'But of course, although I am at a loss to see what advice I can give you, when you have your brother and Maritza.'

'She is too young, both in years and experience, to discuss what troubles me, and Michael's ways are not always mine. When he marries, life will be a combination of heaven and hell for his poor wife. He has so much to give a woman, yet I fear he does not know how. He has been alone too long.'

Alone! As constant companion to the dazzling Catherine! Emma swallowed the natural retort which rose to her lips.

'I think it strange you should ask me for advice,' she answered. He looked worried now. Genuinely troubled by some deep misgivings he had hidden from everyone outside.

'You have lived beneath the same roof as Anne for many years. You are aware of her faults as well as her good points. She will not accept me, Emma.'

'But—but she must. She is your wife.'

'A wife who has locked me out of her room . . . or lain in my arms like a rag doll, tolerating my love-making, but letting me know how she hates every minute of it. I love Anne. I have tried so many ways to make her happy. She accepts the jewels I give her, the clothes, the new carriage and horses, but she refuses to accept I am her husband . . . refuses to accept that at any time I can assert my rights if I choose.'

'Perhaps she is the kind of woman who would prefer her husband to be the master in all things,' Emma returned hesitantly. How could she, not yet twenty years old, who had never known a man, speak with wisdom on such a subject?

'Is she? You know her better than anyone. What must I do? Will nothing satisfy her? Is she homesick, do you think? She is forever talking of her parents and how their absence grieves her. Were they close?'

'Anne was very close to her father,' Emma admitted. 'To be truthful, I think they should have been with her from the very beginning. They should have shared the journey, the wedding, helped her to adjust to the new way of life. They spoiled her terribly, as I suspect you are doing, but when she wants to she can be so . . . enchanting. I know she has felt isolated and alone at times. No-one can take the place of family and friends—not even a husband—not straightaway.' She was thinking of her own mother and father as she spoke, of the years she had missed sharing with them. 'I could write to them . . .'

'Will you? Ask them to visit us in St Petersburg. I will provide whatever expenses are necessary. Needless to say this conversation is between us alone. Michael would not approve of the idea at all. His shoulders are broad, but he cannot cope with everything. He must not be told.'

What worries could Michael Adashev have, Emma wondered, as she nodded agreement. He had several fine houses, rich productive land in the country and he was a favourite at court . . . and somewhere in the background loomed a prospective wife. Did he fear a fall from grace if the Czar removed his erring wife from the throne? The loss of his wealth . . . perhaps even his life?

A shudder ran through her at the thought, and Nikolai frowned in concern.

'Forgive me, I have ruined your evening.' He left his chair and came to stand beside her. He took her hand and touched it to his lips. 'Thank you for listening so patiently.'

'I will write to Lord Tarrant tomorrow,' Emma promised.

'You shall have a letter of credit against my bank first thing. Assure them they will want for nothing while they are here.'

'I will.'

He was still holding her hand when the door opened and Michael sauntered in.

'So this is where you are hiding yourself,' Michael drawled. He was addressing himself to his brother, but his gaze was on Emma and the blue eyes were like chips of ice. 'You promised Andrei Koustev a game of cards. He has been looking for you for the past ten minutes.'

'Good, that will un-nerve him sufficiently to enable me to win,' Nikolai returned with a chuckle. 'I have told Emma about Annushka. She is very upset. Keep her here for a while longer, Michael.'

As the door closed behind him Michael swung round on the chair where Emma sat, his mouth tightening into a bleak line.

'My brother's concern for you is most touching.'

The firelight flickered across her pale cheeks as she stood up to offer the apology she knew he was expecting. The words stuck in her throat and the look on his face grew almost contemptuous.

'Why are you at a loss, mademoiselle? You were not so unsure of yourself at Malayevka—or closeted here alone with my brother . . .'

The insinuation brought a stab of pain to her heart. She deserved his scorn, had steeled herself to receive it the moment he stepped into the room. But not this . . .

'Just what do you think you were interrupting, sir?' she demanded stiffly. 'Your brother brought me in here to break the terrible news about Annushka. Why did you not tell me yourself? Why did you allow me to . . . to . . .'

'To insult me?' Michael snapped. 'Because I was foolishly under the impression you had come to care for the girl and by keeping the truth from you I was saving you grief.'

'I was fond of her,' Emma said, her voice faltering. 'And I was wrong to say the things I did. Please accept my apology.'

He cut across her almost inaudible words with a fierce expletive.

'If you dare to voice your misguided opinions openly again you might well see me turn into the devil you take for granted is in my nature. Concern yourself with my sister and stay out of matters which are none of your business. And I suggest you make your interest in my brother less obvious by finding yourself another companion for the remainder of the evening. Women! My God, I shall never understand what motives lie behind some of the irresponsible things they do.'

'Your brother, sir, is the only person who made me feel welcome when I arrived in Russia. I am still Anne's poor relation and always will be. She has made sure of that here tonight. I doubt if there is one person out there who does not know of my circumstances, how my thoughtful cousin prevailed upon you to engage me as your sister's companion so that I would have security for the rest of my days.' She gave a bitter laugh. 'What a fool I was to believe it could be different. If you will excuse me, I think I will do as you suggest. I am sure there is one man here tonight who will not mind dancing with one of the lower classes.'

Picking up her skirts, she swept past him, her head held high. When he came after her into the ballroom, she was in the arms of an amorous youngster who was still attempting to persuade her to meet him later at one of the hunting lodges which dotted the estate. She looked as if she was enjoying herself with her black hair swirling about her shoulders, laughing softly as her partner bent to whisper yet another meaningless endearment in her ear. How could he know the agony in her heart as he strode past without a second glance, the longing to have his strong arms about her, his lips against her cheek . . . ?

Emma wrote to the Tarrants the following morning and had just finished the letter when a messenger from Belmaya arrived and was shown into her sitting-room. He gave her the letter of credit Nikolai had promised, together with a request to give her letter to his messenger who would then convey it in all speed to the nearest port of departure. 'I want nothing to delay their arrival,' Nikolai had written. Emma was in full agreement with that sentiment.

She followed the messenger downstairs and then froze in dismay as Michael came in from his morning ride. His gaze followed the man out through the front door and then he turned and stared at her questioningly.

'I—I have had a letter from Anne . . . she wishes to make up our quarrel,' Emma lied, and turned and went back to her room before he could question her further.

An answer came from England on the 26th April. Not only had the Tarrants accepted Nikolai's offer, but Emma realised, from the date of the letter that they were already well on their way. If there were no delays they would reach St Petersburg within the next three weeks. Excitedly she penned a short note to Nikolai enclosing the letter and sent it immediately to Belmaya with strict instructions it was to be given into his hands alone.

In one corner of the garden she had found an arbour where wild honeysuckle and roses bloomed in the spring sunshine. It had become her favourite place and when there was nothing else for her to do and the sun was shining she would take a book and hide herself away for a few hours. The following afternoon, her gown finished, Emma declined to go riding with Maritza, took a book from the library and went outside.

Nikolai found her there some time later, so engrossed in what she was reading that she was unaware of his presence until a shadow suddenly fell over the pages and she looked up, startled.

'Good afternoon. Have you come to see your brother? I'm afraid he is not here. I think he is still at Peterhof.'

'He is about ten minutes behind me with Anne and Maritza. He stopped at Belmaya on his way home and decided to come hunting with us. Emma, sweet little cousin, how can I ever thank you for what you have done?'

'I, too, am glad they are coming,' Emma replied, colour rising in her cheeks at his words. 'Have you told Anne?'

'Not yet. She is in the foulest of moods this morning . . . about nothing to wear for the Czarina's ball tomorrow. I have decided to tell her at the last moment. Her parents can stay as long as they wish if it will make her happy.'

It would make Anne happy, but displease Michael, Emma thought.

'You must never tell Anne I played any part in this. She might resent the fact you confided in me, Prince Nikolai . . .'

'Nikolai,' he corrected with a smile. 'Are we not related by marriage? I will not continue this farce any longer. You are part of the Adashev family, do you understand?'

'If—if you insist.' She could think of nothing but how Michael would react to her addressing his brother so intimately.

'I do. Goodbye, little cousin.' He bent and brushed her cheek with his lips.

Emma rose to her feet, not wishing to linger and perhaps encounter Michael upon his return. She saw the smile abruptly vanish from Nikolai's face. Three figures stood at the end of the path. One was his brother. The others were Anne and Maritza.

'Did I not tell you,' she heard Anne's shrill voice ring out accusingly. 'Look at them . . .'

'That is enough!' The cold mask which settled over Nikolai's face, the harshness of his tone, silenced Anne. For a moment she stared at him, huge tears brimming in her eyes. Then with a toss of her red curls, she wheeled about and ran.

'Go after her,' Michael snapped. 'And you, Maritza, into the house. I wish to speak to mademoiselle Fraser alone.'

The order defied argument. With a frosty stare at Emma, the girl hurried past. It was obvious she believed the worst. What had Anne been saying to them both? Nikolai stood his ground, prepared to defend her, Emma realised. She laid a hand on his arm. If he did, he would ruin everything.

'Please go, Nikolai,' she whispered.

'Perhaps you are right. Anne rides like a mad woman when she is angry. You and I will talk later, Michael.'

Emma turned towards the house, but in two long strides, Michael was in front of her, blocking the way.

'You are not going to escape that easily, mademoiselle and before you open that pretty little mouth to feed me more lies, I think you should know Anne knows nothing of the letter you were supposed to have sent her. You wrote to my brother, did you not?' When Emma did not answer, her wrist was seized by his lean fingers, and so fierce was his grip she cried out in pain. 'Tell me the truth, damn you. Has my brother communicated with you since that night at Belmaya?'

'Yes.' She raised her head and looked into his angry face. Defiance blazed out of her eyes.

'And you with him? Yes, you have already admitted that.'

'Of what am I accused?' Emma demanded.

'Of that you are well aware. If I had any sense I would send you packing this instant.'

'It is not what you think . . .' she began and then lapsed into an awkward silence.

'Then why did you lie about the letter? You asked Nikolai to meet you here, didn't you? That's why he pretended his horse's shoe was loose. Do you hate your cousin so much you would deliberately ruin her marriage?'

Emma looked at him as if he had taken leave of his senses. She tried to twist free from his grasp, but he was too strong.

'Be still!' Michael growled, and when she still fought against his grip, suddenly caught both her wrists in one hand, and encircling her waist with his other arm crushed her against his chest. He lowered his head towards her, his eyes glittering at the alarm which leapt to her face. 'You did not have to steal another woman's man. There are plenty of unmarried ones about. For instance—me! It's time you and I came to an understanding.'

Emma averted her face from the mouth intent on seeking hers, brought near to panic by the close contact of his body against hers. Dear God, she thought. He believed she and Nikolai were having an affair!

'Free? You are not free. You belong to the Czarina.' The words were hurled at him in a desperate bid to make him release her. Without a word Michael slapped her across the cheek, and then his mouth sought hers. She was too dazed to offer further resistance as his lips explored hers with an expertise that sent a shiver of fear through her body. He must have felt it, for he drew back instantly. His fingers brushed her smarting cheek and for a moment she thought he was about to apologise. Instead, he said harshly:

'I warned you what would happen the next time we crossed swords. For your own sake, make this the last time.'

Emma fell backwards on to the arbour seat, blinded by tears. When she raised her head again, she was alone.

CHAPTER SEVEN

THE next morning it was obvious that the incident had reached the ears of the servants. Not wanting Maritza to misconstrue the gossip which must surely have reached her, Emma sought her out immediately and acquainted her with the full facts, swearing her to secrecy over the forthcoming visit of the Tarrants.

'Did you enjoy it?' Maritza looked at Emma, her expression positively wicked. 'When Michael kissed you, did you enjoy it?'

'What a question. No, I did not.' It was the first time she had ever been kissed, and it was not the earth-shattering experience of her dreams.

'Have you never been in love?'

'No.'

'Was there no-one in England?'

'I was the impoverished daughter of a titled lady who had married beneath her. I lived on the charity of my aunt and uncle and spent my days at Anne's beck and call,' Emma answered quietly. 'Without a dowry what man would be interested in me?'

'I shall find you a rich husband in Petersburg,' Maritza declared.

'No, thank you. I am quite happy as I am. I must go and change if we are going riding.' Emma rose to her feet and went back to her room before Maritza decided to probe more deeply into her personal life.

Katya dressed her hair that evening, twisting the strands of jet into thick curls on the top of her head and securing them with combs and cream ribbons to match her dress. It fitted perfectly. The neckline with its rich lace collar curved low over her shoulders, but did not reveal as much of her as Catherine's gown had done. The lace and muslin on the sleeves was also threaded with cream ribbon and some of darker velvet to accentuate the delicate colour. As she gazed at herself in the mirror, Emma was well pleased with her efforts.

There was a knock on the door as she was fastening her mother's gold locket around her neck. The maid came to say Prince Adashev was waiting in her sitting-room. Emma's hand trembled as she smoothed a stray curl back into place. Had he come to remonstrate with her still further over her meeting with his brother?

He was standing by the couch, staring down at a piece of embroidery she had been working on earlier. At the rustle of her skirts he turned, with deliberate slowness, Emma thought, and inspected her appearance for a full minute in silence before he said:

'I have just received word from Nikolai. Neither he nor Anne will be coming with us tonight.'

'Is my cousin unwell?' she ventured to ask.

'A slight chill, from what Nikolai says. Nothing serious, but he considers it wiser for her to remain at home. She is naturally disappointed, but there will be other times.' He indicated the locket around her neck. 'Please remove that. You will be wearing this tonight.'

Emma caught her breath at the necklace he took from his pocket. On each side of the enormous ruby were two smaller rubies set in gold, with a diamond between each.

'I cannot, sir,' she protested in a hollow tone and made no move to obey him. 'It—it would not be proper . . .'

'And the English are always so proper, are they not?' he remarked sarcastically. 'You will do as I ask. You are to be presented to the Czarina formally tonight, and you do not want to appear before her as Anne's poor relation, do you?'

The taunt struck home. Without a word she removed the locket and allowed him to replace it with the necklace, steeling herself not to tremble as his fingers brushed her skin.

'Ice and fire, an interesting combination. I wonder which is more dominant in you, Emma Fraser?' He stepped back and gave a nod of satisfaction. 'That should have the desired effect.'

She grew cold at his words. If anyone had picked up snippets of gossip from the ball at Belmaya when she was alone with Nikolai, the sight of her, a mere companion, wearing a fortune in jewels would set their minds working along a much different track.

'I will wear it because I have no other choice.' Emma stood her ground in the face of the mocking smile.

With Nikolai and Anne absent and Michael hovering over her, she knew only too well what people would think—and so did he!

'Soon, very soon, sir, you may have cause to offer an apology to me for the continued insults heaped on my head, for the misinterpretation of innocent actions on my part. You have misunderstood from the very beginning, and judged me unfairly. You, who do not like to be judged by others . . .'

'If that is the case, then you have only to tell me the truth, and if, as you say, I have been wrong, then you shall have your apology this very minute.'

Michael interrupted with a frown. 'I use my eyes. I know what I saw. Good God, girl, I'm not blind!'

'As you wish,' Emma returned.

He followed her when she went to fetch her cloak and gloves. As she passed the dressing table mirror, the lighted candles framed her for a moment in their muted glow. She did not want to look at her reflection, conscious of Michael watching her, but she could not help herself. It was more from curiosity than vanity.

The brilliance of diamonds sparkled between the dull fire of the rubies he had placed against her white skin. She should have felt like a queen with such wealth at her throat, the huge stone nestling just above the rise of her breasts must have been worth a king's ransom. But he had made that impossible. He was using her, and that was the bitterest pill of all.

Michael's reflection appeared in the glass behind her Her cloak was slid around her shoulders. The touch of his fingers was as light as a breath of wind.

'Maritza is in high spirits. It is the first time she has seen Vasily Zouroff in six months. Make sure she does not elude you tonight,' he warned.

Which meant he would be otherwise occupied, with Catherine, Emma thought as she accompanied him downstairs. He wanted to control the lives of those around him, yet did not control his own. His life, and his future, lay in the hands of the Czarina of Russia!

The palace at Peterhof had long been a favourite of Czars and their families, and it proved no exception for Catherine. She had chosen to live in the small summer house of Mon Plaisir, situated in the enormous grounds and close to the sea. Here, where she was less closely watched by her husband's numerous spies and informants, she was able to hold her own court and, most important of all, receive information which would otherwise be denied her.

The Czar Peter was closeted away at Oranienbaum with a following of fawning, scheming followers, drilling his soldiers. He now insisted that those around him openly acknowledged his mistress, Elizabeth Vorontsova, as the future Czarina. On top of this insult, he was talking of having his son, the Grand Duke Paul, declared a bastard and sending his wife to a convent as an adulteress, not realising that the continuous stream of abuse so deliberately directed at her only increased her popularity.

Already there were many on Catherine's side. Not least among them, the Orloff brothers, who had surrounded themselves with the cream of the army officers. There were said to be ten thousand men ready and willing to fight for her.

Not until she entered the long ballroom crowded with people did Emma realise the extent of Catherine's popularity among the army. She had never seen so many colourful uniforms! Bright reds and blues and greens trimmed with gold braid; dark fur-trimmed capes flung carelessly over stalwart shoulders. Highly polished low-slung sabres which might one day be drawn in her defence, gleamed in the candlelight. Emma recognised many faces from the bal masqué at Belmaya, and realised that some of the most important families in St Petersburg were here. This was no casual affair. It was a show of strength in Catherine's favour.

As they stood just inside the doorway, Maritza scanned the people passing by, looking for one face in particular. Michael was greeted by a man in uniform with a scarred cheek, who stared at Emma so boldly she turned away in embarrassment. After a few moments Michael excused himself and the two of them wandered to the other end of the room, where the Czarina sat in a gilded chair, surrounded by men and women all trying to engage her in conversation, each trying to outdo the other for a smile or a favoured word. She sensed an undercurrent of excitement in the room. What was being whispered behind those fluttering fans and white-gloved hands? How best to ingratiate themselves with the woman it was now widely rumoured was about to take over the throne of Russia from her weak-willed husband? On whose side they should stand? For Catherine and a chance of great rewards for their loyalty? Or for the Czar Peter and risk the chance of losing their heads, or at the very least being sent into exile, if he turned against them in one of his very unpredictable moods?

When it was all over, would Michael and his family be held in high esteem by a grateful Empress—or would they all be banished to the snowlands of Siberia, perhaps even confined in the dreaded fortress of St Peter and St Paul? The latter thought made her shiver with fear, and Maritza glanced sideways at her.

'It is all right, Emma, you look very, very lovely.' She had mistaken the shiver for apprehension of the nobility surrounding them. Her eyes rested on the ruby and diamond necklace at the other girl's throat. 'I am glad to see my brother is capable of accepting advice as well as giving it.'

'I'm sorry. I don't understand.'

'I told him how badly he had behaved towards you in the garden and that he should apologise, but words seemed to have failed him. I hope you are pleased with his gift. I did not offer any explanation, you understand, but I made it quite clear what I thought of his behaviour.'

'Gift,' Emma said, in a startled tone. 'He said nothing to me . . . he knows—he knows I could not possibly accept it as a gift. What would people think?'

'Naturally he would not expect you to publicise it all over St Petersburg,' Maritza returned, a tiny frown puckering her brows. 'It is a personal thing, just between the two of you. Besides, he said, without Anne's overbearing presence here tonight, it would be nice if you could at last put out of your mind this feeling of being a—what is it you English say?—a poor relation. You are not, you know. You are part of our family now, Emma, and we will always take care of you. Oh, look! There is Natasha Orlova. I must go and talk to her.'

Before Emma could gather her reeling senses, Maritza had picked up her skirts and disappeared into the crowd. Mindful of Michael's insistence she should remain with his sister at all times, she quickly followed, but the chatter of the two excited girls, which went on as they discussed Natasha's latest beau, and the newest Paris fashions, not to mention the scandalous snippets of court gossip about the Czarina and her newest paramour, Gregory Orloff, passed mostly over Emma's head. She stood beside them lost in her own thoughts, her fingers often straying to the necklace at her throat.

A gift—by way of the apology he obviously found too difficult, or too distasteful to put into words. How eloquently Maritza must have spoken on her behalf. She had misinterpreted Michael's motives, and he had said nothing to alleviate the suspicions he had surely realised were in her mind as he fastened it around her neck. She would return it to him politely but firmly, the moment they returned to Malayevka.

Natasha gave a giggle and leaned forward to whisper something in Maritza's ear. Immediately Emma was on her guard. She followed Maritza's gaze as her head flew up and her eyes became fixed on a slimly-built young man in the uniform of the Czarina's personal guard, who was approaching them. There was an arrogance in his face, despite his youth—Emma imagined he was no more than twenty-two—a swagger to his walk that made many a pretty girl risk a sidelong glance in his direction as he passed by.

Maritza suddenly caught Emma by the hand. She was trembling. As Natasha turned and walked away with another giggle, the officer halted beside them. The boldness of his gaze as he studied Maritza made her blush and lower her eyes.

'Princess, I was hoping you would be here tonight.' He touched the girl's fingers to his lips. They lingered there a moment longer than was necessary.

'Vasily, it is so good to see you again.' Maritza's cheeks were bright pink. Reluctantly she disengaged herself and stepped back, conscious of the many probing eyes around her. 'May I present Emma Fraser, from England, my new companion.'

'Don't you mean watchdog?' Vasily's lip curled in disapproval. 'I heard Michael had found another one.'

'That is not fair,' Maritza protested, and two angry sparks glittered in her eyes. 'You will not speak to Emma that way. She is my friend.'

'Friend? She knows about us?' As Maritza nodded, the young man stared hard into Emma's face and then a smile touched his mouth. 'If you are truly her friend, then I am very pleased we have met and I hope you will also be mine. It would be a comforting thought to at last have someone on our side. Over this past year Michael has done his damnedest to cause a rift between us, either by shutting poor Maritza away in that mausoleum of a house at Malayevka, or having her constantly chaperoned by stony-faced old maids who report back to him on every move she makes.'

Which is exactly what she was expected to do, Emma thought, hating the deception she was forced to practise.

'Am I to be trusted to dance with you—in full view of your new companion, of course,' Vasily asked, tucking Maritza's arm beneath his.

'Don't be silly,' the girl gave a nervous little laugh. 'Emma probably wants to dance herself, don't you?'

'In a while.'

A moment later Michael was at her side, together with the scar-faced man who had been with him since he arrived.

'I see Maritza is determined to make the most of the evening,' he remarked dryly.

'She is only dancing,' Emma protested in a quiet voice. 'What harm can that do? She has not been out of my sight for a moment—nor will she be.'

'Do I read from your tone that you approve of her choice?'

'I thought him pleasant and well-mannered,' she said, determined to make her opinion known for Maritza's sake, 'but I fully realise it is not my place to offer comment.'

'I am glad you make it unnecessary to remind you of your duties. You are my sister's companion, not an adviser on matters of the heart, of which, as you have already told me, you have no knowledge,' Michael returned. The veiled threat told her he would tolerate no interference in this matter.

'When it becomes necessary to remind you of your position, rest assured I shall be the one to do it' . . . Emma's cheeks flamed with colour as his words returned to mock her. She had deliberately chosen her words with care—to no avail it seemed.

'You will never find it necessary, sir,' she said, tight-lipped. In that moment she was not sure which one of the emotions raging inside her was the strongest—love—or hate.

'Now look what you have done. You have embarrassed the child,' Michael's companion said with a deep-throated chuckle. 'Will you never learn the fine arts, Michael my friend. Women do not like harsh words—or to be reminded of their weaknesses.'

He looked at Emma in the same bold manner as before, but this time she did not look away. Child indeed! At the sight of the anger smouldering in her grey eyes, his smile grew. Even with his scarred cheek he was still attractive—typical of the men who seemed to cluster around the Czarina, she thought.

'Will you keep your eye on Maritza—I have to take Mademoiselle Fraser to be presented,' Michael murmured.

'Only on the condition you allow me to have at least one dance with your new acquisition,' came the reply which made Emma bristle even more.

It made her sound like a piece of furniture, she thought indignantly.

'You will find she has a mind of her own.' Michael's mouth crooked into an amused smile. 'I suggest you ask her yourself.'

'I regret I shall have little time for dancing . . .' Emma began, but her protest was waved aside.

'I will seek you out for the next mazurka. Now, where is that delightful sister of yours, Michael?'

'Yonder, by the window. Watch over her well, Alexei. She is not to be alone with Zouroff for a moment.'

'The young pup still refuses to heed your warnings, I see. Faith, but you've been patient with him. Perhaps the flat of your blade might prove a more successful inducement.'

'In time perhaps. Come, mademoiselle.'

Emma placed her hand on the arm Michael offered and allowed herself to be led the whole length of the room to where Catherine sat. She caught her breath as she had her first clear view of the Czarina since her arrival.

Catherine's gown was a magnificent creation of black

velvet and satin, slashed low across her full breasts and heavily encrusted with priceless jewels. The deep lustre of emeralds glowed against the creamy whiteness of her skin. She looked more beautiful than the last time Emma had seen her.

Her thoughts flew back to that afternoon at Malayevka, to the memory of Catherine relaxing back onto the couch and the open pelisse which had inadvertently betrayed the fact she was carrying a child. She was not pregnant now. Her tiny waist was likely to be the envy of every woman in the room. Once again the identity of the father rose up to haunt her. Was it one of the many officers she had so carefully cultivated since the death of Elizabeth Petrovna—or the latest of her lovers, Gregory Orloff, who stood at her side a hand resting casually along the back of her chair. Maritza had pointed him out to Emma.

He bore a striking resemblance to the scar-faced man, but was taller and his features more distinctive. From beneath strong brows, large eyes surveyed those around him, with an expression which almost bordered on indifference, as if he was wishing everyone would leave so that he could be alone with the Czarina. She noticed the mouth was full and sensuous as he bent his head to whisper in Catherine's ear.

Emma felt Michael's fingers curl tightly around hers as she swept down in a deep curtsey and when she rose, found his eyes were locked on her face. Had she betrayed her thoughts, even for a moment?

'I am pleased to see you again, Emma Fraser,' Catherine said, nodding in her direction. 'Bring her closer, Michael. Let me look at her. Yes, a definite improvement since we last met. I think my country suits you, does it not?'

'Yes, indeed, Your Imperial Majesty,' Emma replied, conscious of many eyes turned curiously in her direction.

'And are you happy in your new position with the Adashev household?'

What could she say, with Michael holding tightly to

her hand, his eyes still intent on her face? She had never been happier anywhere else—or so miserable.

'I am most grateful the Prince has made it possible for me to remain in Russia after my cousin's marriage,' she replied.

Amusement flickered across Catherine's face, but if she read another meaning into the reply, she made no comment on it.

She rose to her feet as the musicians struck up another polonaise.

'I think it is time I danced. We will talk again later.'

Immediately there were a dozen eager men hovering in her path, but she had eyes for only one. With a warm smile she turned to the uniformed figure at her side and placed her hand in his in such a possessive manner Emma found herself glancing up at the silent man at her side, waiting for his reaction. Michael's features registered no emotion. How painful this new liaison must be to him, she thought, stepping back to allow the couple to pass. He would never know that this was a painful moment for her too—seeing him so vulnerable . . .

If only she did not care! If only she could shut him out of her mind, her life. But neither was possible. Her mother had loved but one man, and with Emma it would be the same. They would continue to argue and one of them would, invariably, lose control. He would mock and taunt her in the months to come, and there would be times when she would hate him, but it had taken this evening to prove just how deep and strong her love was. No matter what he said, or how callous his behaviour, she would stay beneath his roof, because she loved him. He would never know it—but there might come a time when he needed to unburden himself, as Nikolai had done. How could she ever have thought of leaving when he might need her . . .

'Would you like to dance?'

'Yes, please.'

What did it matter if she took second place because

the woman he really wanted was in someone else's arms? His would be holding her and that was all that mattered just now, Emma thought, as she allowed him to guide her onto the floor.

When the music changed to a mazurka, immediately the scar-faced man appeared to claim Emma for his dance.

'Tell me, where did you find this charming creature?' he remarked.

'Save your compliments, Alexei. Mademoiselle Fraser is English and I assure you English people are immune to flattery,' Michael answered, moving aside.

'No woman is immune to flattery, my friend. You obviously lack the finesse needed to bring this beautiful flower to blossom. Mademoiselle Fraser, allow me to introduce myself as Michael here is loath to do so. I am Alexei Orloff.'

Gregory's brother! One of the five close-knit Orloff's who had openly proclaimed their support for Catherine's cause.

'Behave yourself, Alexei,' Michael growled quietly. 'She is not one of your women. Give her cause for complaint and I'll put a scar on the other cheek.'

Emma caught her breath, expecting an angry retort, yet to her surprise Alexei threw back his head and bellowed with laughter.

'You are the last person I would cross swords with, my friend. She will be safe with me, I swear it. You are not pleased to be parted from my friend Michael,' Alexei remarked as he led Emma breathless from the dance-floor some while later and headed them in the direction of the punch table. 'I cannot blame you. He is one of the most eligible men here tonight . . . although I have heard a rumour he has his eye on some mysterious woman with a view to marriage. Poor girl, she will have her hands full with that one.'

'You are a close friend of the Prince?' Emma asked.

'We were in the same regiment. After the death of his father, some two years ago, he asked permission from the late Empress to resign his commission and devote all his time to his estates, and she granted his wish. A pity; he was a good fighter.'

'He did not like the life?'

Emma sipped her glass of hot, spiced punch, deliberating on Michael Adashev the soldier—a man she had never known.

'Some of us are born to it. Others, like Michael, have a higher calling. But that is enough of him. I want to hear all about you.'

'I am sorry, but I cannot stay.' Emma had been searching the room for several minutes and was worried to find Maritza was missing. So too was Vasily Zouroff. Michael would be furious!

'Now what have I said to frighten you away?' Alexei asked. 'Don't worry about Michael, he is otherwise occupied just now.'

Emma's eyes flew across the room. There was no sign of Catherine, or Gregory Orloff or Michael. Conscious of the smile on the face of her companion, she declined the offer of wine and stepped back, saying in a firm voice:

'Thank you for the dance, but I must find Maritza . . .'

'My dear girl she will not be pleased if you interrupt her while she is with Zouroff. Why risk her displeasure? Stay with me . . . we will look for her together later on.'

Michael's displeasure would be far more terrible than any angry words Maritza might toss her way, Emma thought with a determined shake of her head.

'Please excuse me.'

She spun around on her heel, Alexei Orloff forgotten as she began a desperate search of the room. There was no sign of her charge anywhere.

In fact, as she looked slowly and very carefully around the room, Emma realised many women stood alone, their uniformed escorts conspicuous by their absence. Her first suspicions had been correct. Everyone present tonight had been summoned for a reason. The Czarina was counting her loyal followers. Emma cared nothing for the others. But Michael!

She pushed him ruthlessly to the back of her mind. He was quite able to take care of himself, but he had placed his sister's welfare in her hands—and she had failed in her duty.

Her sympathy was with Maritza, not her strong-willed, over-dominant brother who held sway over so many lives. She would not mention the deliberate disobedience of his instructions, if only she could find the girl before he became aware of her absence.

Emma looked for her in the garden and found herself politely, but very firmly having to deter the attentions of a young cavalryman who had followed her outside. By the time she had made it quite clear she neither wanted to dance nor make a date for supper after the ball, she was growing considerably agitated.

There was no sign of Maritza and her companion anywhere. She was wondering if she dared attempt to look the other side of the maze of mirrored doors which made up the Great Hall, when one of them opened and several uniformed men stepped out and hurried quickly in the direction of the ballroom. A moment later four more followed.

Emma pressed herself back into one of the shadowy alcoves which lined the long, dimly lighted corridor to her rear, the moment she recognised Michael Adashev. He was frowning as he listened intently to something Gregory Orloff was telling him. He was so engrossed Emma doubted if he would have noticed her if she had stood in his very path.

There had been some kind of meeting of all the army officers, she realised, and, of course, Vasily Zouroff, in his capacity as one of the Czarina's guard, would be there too. She had been worrying for nothing. Maritza was very likely upstairs refreshing herself, or gossiping with one of the many girl friends she had not seen over the past months.

Silly idiot! You could have been enjoying yourself instead of getting into an unnecessary state of nerves, she thought. She lingered for a moment longer in the shadows to compose herself before following in the footsteps of the stream of uniformed figures.

She had taken but one step from the alcove when she heard the sound of voices approaching behind her and turned. The candlelight illuminated her features as she stepped out further and the first man, who almost blundered into her in the dimness, gave a sharp oath and immediately changed direction to go back the way he had come. But not before she had been scrutinised by a pair of narrowed eyes which, for some reason, sent a cold chill down her spine.

The sudden movement knocked a pouch from the hands of his companion. The heavy chink of coins as it hit the floor told her it contained a large amount of money. It was scooped up without a word and the man hurried off.

'My dear Mademoiselle Fraser, are you lost by any chance?' Vasily Zouroff asked, moving to her side. She was taken purposefully by the arm and propelled towards the open door of the ballroom.

The firmness of his grip, the annoyance registering in his tone, despite his smile, indicated he was angry to have come upon her. Why had he not been at the meeting and why was his companion so disturbed at being seen.

'I was looking for Maritza,' Emma replied, disengaging herself.

'I am about to take her home. There is no need for you to be concerned any longer.'

'On the contrary you have just given me reason,' she insisted. 'I cannot allow you to escort her unless I accompany you.'

'So you are Michael's spy after all,' Vasily sneered.

The pleasant smile became a derisive mask and an undisguised menacing undercurrent invaded the previously friendly tone of voice. He did not care if Michael followed them, she realised. It was almost as if he wanted it.

'In a very short time Maritza and I will be married. There is nothing her brother can do about it now, and if you know what is good for you, Emma Fraser, I suggest you change sides while you have the chance. Maritza would be very generous in the future to anyone who helped her during this difficult time—and you would be useful to me too. She is under the impression you have taken Michael's eye.' He laughed softly at the indignation rising in Emma's face. He was suggesting she betrayed Michael's trust . . . something she had contemplated and dismissed as impossible less than an hour ago. The knowledge filled her with a deep sense of shame. She would have allowed Maritza to be alone with the man she loved and remained silent. She knew now, that would have been totally wrong.

When she had first met Vasily Zouroff, she found him exactly as Maritza had described him—a young, handsome courteous soldier she had known for the past twelve months, who had swept her off her feet with his deep declaration of love and devotion. It had been the description of a woman in love, as blind as any other woman in the same position, to the faults of the person she adored. Michael, on the other hand, immune to soft words of flattery, had looked beneath the surface charm and discovered something he did not like, something which had instantly set him against any liaison between this man and his sister.

Surely Vasily realised, by taking Maritza home, unchaperoned, and without her brother's permission, he was being deliberately provoking. An unpleasant scene, possibly a fight, even a duel might result from his foolish disregard for convention.

'I must insist I return with you to Malayevka,' Emma said, in an icy tone. 'Or I shall have no alternative but to go to Prince Michael. He will stop you.'

'Have the English no romance in their souls? No, I shall not allow you to accompany us. Run to Michael, if you can find him, that is. These occasions bore him to such an extent he usually persuades the Czarina to a game of cards somewhere quiet. Disturb him if you dare, and be damned to you both. I promise you will regret your interference in my affairs.'

He moved towards the main doors. As a servant swung them open Emma had a brief glimpse of a closed carriage waiting outside and Maritza's anxious face framed at the window, before she moved quickly back out of sight. Michael! She had to find Michael!

He was at one of the supper tables with a group of officers, Alexei Orloff and his brothers among them, looking more relaxed than she had seen him in many weeks.

'Mademoiselle Fraser, my irresistible charm has brought you back to my side, like a moth to a candle flame,' Alexei remarked and his words brought laughter from several of his companions. He was obviously a well-known ladies' man.

'Please, may I speak with you. It is very important.' Emma ignored Alexei—she had eyes only for Michael.

'You have lost out tonight, Alexei. She prefers Michael,' someone joked as Michael excused himself, took her by the arm and escorted her out onto the deserted patio. He said not one word until they were alone.

'What is it? You are trembling.'

She tried to withdraw from his grasp, but he held her fast, demanding again:

'What is it?'

'Captain Zouroff has insisted on taking your sister home alone. He would not let me go with them.' The words tumbled out in a rush. His face was in the shadows, but she was able to imagine the anger there, heard it rising in his voice as he snapped:

'When was this?'

'Only a few minutes ago. He had a carriage waiting.'

She was abruptly released and left standing on the long verandah, with the sound of the sea pounding in her ears as it hammered against the rocky cliffs a hundred yards away. Michael strode purposefully in the direction of the stables.

'Wait.' She ran past well-tended flower beds, around carved stone fountains which sent water spiralling into the air over her head, to catch up with him. He ignored her and called loudly for Jan to bring the carriage. 'Please.'

'And let them get away?' He wheeled on her, eyes blazing. 'Damnation! You have made it plain on which side of the fence you are, my loyal English miss . . .'

'No, you don't understand . . .' Emma cried. 'Don't ask me to explain, because I can't, but I have this strange feeling he wants you to follow him. I felt it—heard it in his voice. As if he wishes a confrontation. Though what good it will do him I cannot imagine.'

'Then he will have his wish—on both counts—and he'll rue the day he ever crossed my path. Go back to Mon Plaisir and tell Alexei he is to take you home.'

'I am coming with you—this is partly my fault.' Emma stood her ground. 'Don't you see what he is trying to do? If you catch up with him in this angry mood and there is a fight, Maritza will never forgive you. It will be your fault if she turns against you.'

'No,' Michael returned bleakly, 'it will be yours. I will hold you personally responsible if anything like that happens tonight . . .'

'I—I'm sorry . . .'

The apoology which rose to her lips was never allowed to be spoken. As the carriage rolled to a halt before them, Michael lifted her from the ground and pushed her none too gently inside and then sprang in beside her. Then, with Jan whipping the horses to a furious pace, they sped away from the palace towards the forest road which led to Malayevka.

CHAPTER EIGHT

THE carriage lurched unsteadily over uneven ground and seemed to poise precariously in the air for a terrifying moment before coming back to earth with a bone-shaking jolt which brought a cry to Emma's lips as she was thrown against the door.

In the opposite seat Michael was lost in deep thought, oblivious to her discomfort.

'I did not ask you to come,' he growled as she sat rubbing a bruised wrist.

'No, you did not, but in your present state of mind, I thought someone should be with you,' she flung back with sudden spirit. She was cold and frightened. Not only of her companion, but of the events of the evening which seemed to be pushing them all towards some terrible confrontation.

'Save your sympathy for Zouroff.'

'When I first met him I did not realise . . .'

'That behind that boyish charm and winning smile lay the devious mind of a very ambitious young man?' Michael interrupted her in mid-sentence. 'Zouroff was born the wrong side of the blanket, the son of a titled aristocrat and a peasant woman. He means to achieve the wealth and power denied him by his real father by any means open to him, and I believe that includes marriage to my sister. She is a pawn in his little game, nothing more.'

Emma shivered at the thought of innocent Maritza being duped by the smooth-tongued poison Vasily Zouroff had poured into her ear. Already she resented Michael separating them, forcing her to stay at Malayevka, to brood, to remember, to plan a way to deceive and triumph over her own brother. If Michael acted rashly tonight it could tip the scales against him, throw her perhaps for good into the arms of a man who did not love her—and unwittingly give him the power and status he sought.

Michael's love for his sister would ensure she was well cared for, even if she did marry without his consent. He would be forced to swallow his pride and accept a man he detested into the family, forget the feud between them, for her sake.

Emma shivered again, this time with the cold. She had left her cloak at Mon Plaisir and even though the day had been sunny and warm, a chilling wind had sprung up the moment darkness fell. Reaching into a corner, Michael tossed a fur cloak across to her. She huddled inside it in a grateful silence.

Her eyes widened in alarm as he produced a brace of pistols from a hidden compartment beneath his seat and, after checking them over thoroughly, placed one inside his jacket, the other on the seat beside him.

'Surely you will not need those,' she said in a hollow tone.

'If your concern is for me, it is touching, but misplaced. I have no need of it.'

'My concern is for your sister,' she insisted. 'Please—please do nothing in haste. Whatever happens tonight, she will be the only one hurt . . .'

'You should have thought of that earlier. If you had been watching her . . .'

'It was not my fault your persistent friend Alexei Orloff insisted on dancing with me. I did not want to, if you remember.'

'Few women can resist Alexei when he sets out to have his own way,' Michael said. 'I do not blame you for wanting to enjoy yourself, that is why I took you after all, but for allowing your heart to rule your head. Why are all women such scatterbrains? There is not one among you who isn't deceived by first impressions.'

Emma was about to refute such an unfair statement

when she remembered how Michael had met her in the inn outside St Petersburg. His attire and manner had proclaimed him a servant and she had accepted that was what he was without question.

The carriage came to an abrupt halt. Totally unprepared, Emma was flung bodily out of her seat and against Michael's chest. For a moment her face rested so close to his she could feel his breath against her hair, the sudden quickening of his heartbeats . . . and then he was lifting her away from him and reaching for his pistol.

Jan's face appeared at the window and he used sign language to indicate to his master what had brought them to such an unexpected halt. Emma knew that it had been Michael who had spent hours of painstaking labour teaching the lad how to communicate—in such a way, she found, that only the two of them understood it.

'There is a tree across the road. Stay here while we move it,' Michael ordered, climbing out.

Emma leaned out through the open door. One of the horses shied nervously and Jan went to calm it while Michael walked slowly, and rather cautiously, she thought, towards the object blocking their path. The moon came out of heavy cloud and illuminated a gnarled old tree-trunk lying half way across the road.

This delay would cost Michael precious time, she realised, and a soft sigh of relief escaped her. Perhaps it was a good omen. With any luck Vasily Zouroff would have the good sense to leave Malayevka the moment he had seen Maritza safely inside. They would never meet . . .

The sharp crack which broke the stillness of the night momentarily froze her in horror. She heard a muffled groan and saw Michael stumble and fall. A shadowy figure came rushing out of the bushes behind him. She screamed a warning—and Michael seemed to roll to one side, coming up onto his knees as he did so. Moonlight glinted on the polished barrel of the pistol in his hand, there was another loud discharge and the would-be assassin crashed to the ground in front of him.

Throwing aside the heavy cloak, Emma jumped from the carriage and, running to his side, tried to lift him. She felt something warm and sticky begin to trickle down over one hand.

'Oh, you are hurt . . .' She fought against the faintness which threatened to engulf her.

'Get back into the carriage, you little fool, there may be more of them.' His face contorting with pain, Michael dragged himself to his feet, thrusting her away from him.

'No, I won't leave you,' Emma cried. 'Put your arm around my waist. Jan, try to move the tree . . . hurry! Hurry!'

'He can't manage—he's not strong enough—it will take all of us,' Michael groaned as the boy put all his weight behind the huge object—to no avail.

With Emma's help he tried to walk, but after only a few steps he gave a groan and fell to his knees again.

'Try again,' Emma begged. Perhaps the obstruction was not the good omen she had hoped for, giving Michael's temper time to cool, but was a deliberate attempt on someone's part to slow his progress for a more ominous reason. Someone had tried to kill him!

As she attempted to pull him upright, there was suddenly another figure beside them. Not Jan, whose back was towards them, all his attention centred on the tree-trunk, but a menacing figure whose pistol, levelled at Michael's head, curtailed the scream which rose to her lips. She shrank back with a sharp intake of breath as she looked into the eyes which surveyed them. She had experienced the same chill of fear when they had scrutinised her at Mon Plaisir a short time ago.

'You have a habit of being in the wrong place at the wrong time, mademoiselle.' The man looked down at her pitilessly and she knew he was going to kill her.

'Damn you, no! It's me you want,' Michael broke in harshly and with a tremendous effort he thrust himself between them so that his body shielded hers completely. 'Let her go.'

'To finger me at the first opportunity? You make a

good pair, Prince Adashev. Had I not seen her myself tonight, I would never have suspected this English girl of being your accomplice.'

'What—what does he mean?' Emma asked faintly. Her life was being threatened and she had no idea why.

'Don't be afraid,' Michael turned, one hand coming to rest gently on her shoulder, while, momentarily obscured from view, his other hand sought the second pistol hidden inside his jacket. A look warned her to remain silent.

He wheeled suddenly, but the surreptitious move had been seen and with a vicious kick the man sent the weapon flying. Another kick sent Michael sprawling backwards onto the ground. Emma went down on her knees to support him.

'For that she dies first—and you will watch,' came the bloodcurdling threat and his weapon was turned in her direction.

The smile which twisted his face became unexpectedly a look of surprise, and then in the final moment one of agony, before he fell face down before her with the hilt of Jan's knife protruding from between his shoulder blades.

Emma swayed and would have fallen had Michael's arms not caught and supported her. She turned her face against his chest, her eyes tightly closed, seized with a bout of uncontrollable shivering. He held her close in silence. She needed no words of comfort, the feel of his arms about her was sufficient.

'Can you stand now?' After a moment he held her away from him. Blood had smeared her beautiful gown and he gave an exclamation when he saw it.

'It doesn't matter,' she whispered. 'We are still alive.'

'Thanks to your warning I managed to get one of them at least.'

'But why?' The panic was receding. Questions were beginning to crowd into her mind. 'What did he mean about me being your accomplice?'

'Not now, little Emma.' Michael laid a finger against her lips. Slowly, but firmly she was pulled to her feet by Jan, who then slipped an arm beneath his master's shoulder and, with her help, got him upright. Where Michael's strength came from Emma did not know, but in the moments which followed, he used the strength of his good shoulder, together with what little effort she could put into it, to help the boy move the tree from across the road, before dragging himself up onto one of the carriage seats.

They had been barely fifteen minutes from Malayevka, Emma realised as the carriage came to a halt before the house, the longest moments of her life. Michael refused to allow her to examine his wound, assuring her it was only a flesh wound and she was forced to sit opposite him in an agony of frustration until the lights of the house heralded their safe arrival. Any moment she had expected another attack.

Servants came rushing out to aid their master who reeled towards the steps, blood streaming from his head now as well as soaking through the sleeve of his velvet coat. The last fall had reopened the wound inflicted in the fight with Annushka's attacker Emma saw, as she hurried ahead of them, sending open-mouthed, wide-eyed maids scurrying in all directions for hot water and towels to be brought to the drawing-room. Jan hovered only a few feet away at all times, a silent, protective sentinel, looking for all the world as if he was prepared to slit the throat of anyone careless enough to cause his precious master more pain.

To Emma's relief there had been no sign of another carriage and the upstairs windows were in darkness, which confirmed her suspicions that Maritza had considered it wiser to go directly to bed than wait up for her brother after her scandalous behaviour. Had she known he was following, that is. If Vasily was using her, then he could not afford to make any stupid mistakes which might jeopardise his carefully laid plans. At all times he would have to appear to Maritza as the maligned party, aware of Michael's disapproval, but not understanding it.

'Please remain here until I return.' Michael halted in the doorway, waving aside the servant who was attempting to guide him to a chair. His mouth was taut with pain and his left arm now hung limply at his side, but he was in full control of himself and she marvelled at the supreme effort which kept him on his feet. 'We will talk when I have been upstairs. Jan, fetch mademoiselle something to drink. She must need it.'

He was going to see Maritza, but whether to question, or chastise her, Emma did not know. She did not attempt to interfere. Vasily Zouroff was no love-sick boy who had had an argument with the brother of the girl he wanted to marry. He had cold-bloodedly attempted murder to gain what he wanted. He was treacherous and dangerous and Maritza had to be protected from him. Besides, at that moment, her sole concern was to attend to Michael's injuries.

'Please let me send for a doctor . . .'

'Until I get to the bottom of what happened tonight, I think the fewer people who are involved the better, don't you agree? Maritza's name must never be linked with what took place.'

'The servants . . .' Emma began. She was in full agreement with that. He had been through enough without having his sister's good name sullied by vicious gossip mongers.

'Are loyal to me—every last man and woman in this house. They will talk and speculate among themselves, but it will go no further than these walls, of that I am certain. However, when need be, Jan is my eyes and my ears and I shall know if there are any indiscreet whisperings, and they will be dealt with severely,' Michael replied before leaving her.

Jan the protector, the watchful spy who prowled the corridors of Malayevka like a shadow and was considered unimportant because he could not speak! Had he watched her in the past, Emma wondered, reporting back her every movement? No doubt that was how Michael had first learned of her correspondence with Nikolai.

Now that she was safe, the full realisation of what had almost happened overwhelmed her and she slid down onto the nearest chair as her legs threatened to give way beneath her. She raised her head from between her hands as someone touched her lightly on the shoulder and she found Jan holding out a glass of wine. There was no resentment in her as she took it and drank—only gratitude. If he had been set to watch her, it was no longer important. He had saved her life as well as Michael's.

'Thank you for what you did, Jan. I will never be able to repay you.'

The young lad stared long and hard into her face. She knew full well that he understood what she said, but for a moment his expression remained impassive, the eyes void of all emotion, which was his usual countenance. Except briefly—when he had killed Michael's would-be assassin—then, she remembered, his eyes had blazed with a murderous fury.

Slowly, as if aware she did not understand the adept way he used his hands to communicate, Jan looked around him, then pointed, first to a painting of Michael Adashev in the uniform of a Major in the Preobrazhensky regiment which hung over the fireplace, before motioning in the direction of the bowl of water and towels which had been left on a side table, touching first his shoulder and then his head. He was indicating he wanted her to take care of his master's injuries, she realised, and nodded vigorously.

'Yes, yes, I want to look after him. If only you knew . . .'

She broke off. There was nothing wrong with Jan's hearing and she was afraid the tremor in her voice would betray her deep concern.

Getting to her feet, she replaced her empty glass on the oak sideboard and, in doing so, caught sight of herself in the ornamental mirror hung low behind it. Strands of hair, broken loose from the tight curls, trailed past a face devoid of all colour. The delicate lace fichu she had created with such loving care had a large rent in it where she had caught it on a twig while trying to move the tree-trunk with the others. Her gown was streaked with blood and dirt where she had knelt on the ground beside Michael and he had held her in his arms in those moments after the terrible ordeal was over.

Only the magnificent necklace at her throat remained untouched by what had happened. In the morning she would return it to him. No, better to do so now, before she had time to reflect on Maritza's surprising revelation that it had been meant as a gift and was hers to keep.

With trembling fingers she unfastened it and placed it beside a slender jade figurine.

'Jan, go and find Prince Michael. He should be resting.' Her head was beginning to ache and to be able to stretch out in her own bed upstairs in the quiet of her room was an inviting thought.

'Rest,' Michael repeated from the doorway. He had discarded his coat and replaced it with a brocade robe, belted over his dirt-stained breeches. 'Before I can rest I need the answers to a good many questions,' he added, moving towards the decanters on the sideboard. As usual Jan anticipated his need and poured out a large glass of brandy which Michael accepted with an appreciative nod.

'First, please let me attend to your arm,' Emma pleaded. 'You were bleeding so fiercely.'

'A flesh wound, as I told you,' Michael returned. 'It looked worse that it is. I have experienced more severe injuries in the field.'

'Your head, then . . .'

'Very well, and while you are ministering to me you can do a little explaining. Well, what is it now?' He wheeled about with an impatient expletive as Maritza's maid appeared at the door, an anxious look on her face.

'The Princess is calling for you, Highness—most insistently,' she said falteringly.

'No-one is to go near her without my permission—make that clear to everyone. You have not heard her. Go to bed.'

'What—what have you done?' Emma asked as the woman scurried away.

'I have locked Maritza in her room and there she will remain until I am ready to talk to her. I am in no mood to bandy pleasantries at the moment.' Michael eased himself into a chair and she began to bathe the bloody gash over his temple. The scar, not yet properly healed from his recent fight, had reopened in this latest confrontation. He grimaced just once as she smoothed away some strands of dark hair which had become matted in the wound, but otherwise he betrayed no sign of the discomfort she knew she must be causing him.

'Maritza cannot be held in any way responsible for what has happened tonight.' Emma stood back from his chair, drying her hands on a towel.

'I am aware of that. Nor do I blame you any longer. You must forget what I said earlier. I spoke hastily—and in anger. I asked too much that you be both her friend and her watch-dog. You are not that devious. But concern for her welfare has pushed me towards a situation I know I can no longer handle alone,' Michael replied with an honesty which took her aback. 'I ask only one thing from you in the future, as far as my sister is concerned, and it is that you trust my judgment. Never doubt that I have her best interests at heart, however strange my actions may appear to you. Watch over her for me as if her very life is at stake—even more so after tonight.'

'What is there about Vasily Zouroff she does not know?' If only he would confide in her. Surely there was some way she could help?

'Many things, and she would believe none of them. If I was to tell you he intends to destroy the House of Adashev, what would you say?'

'One man? Against you—and Nikolai? Against the power of the Czarina?' Emma returned. The idea was preposterous. Michael possessed both power and money; Vasily had neither.

Michael leaned his head against the back of his chair, his eyes narrowing as he perceived the incredulity his question had brought to her face.

'And if Catherine cannot help me? What if the Czar is in full control, not playing at being a ruler as he is at the moment?' He broke off. 'No. I have no right to involve you further. Through my own carelessness we were both almost killed tonight. I will not subject you to such dangers again. Tell me of this man tonight. How did you come to know him?'

His tone changed, commanding an answer. Emma knew her many questions would remain unanswered for the time being.

'I did not know him exactly—not even his name. We bumped into each other in the corridor while I was looking for Maritza. He was with Captain Zouroff. Neither were very pleased to see me.'

'Corridor? What corridor—where?' He was beginning to sound like the Grand Inquisitor!

'In the Great Hall.'

'And exactly what did you see?' Michael demanded and she knew it was useless to try and evade the truth.

'You—with Alexei Orloff and his brothers—and other officers, leaving what seemed to be some kind of a meeting. I knew you would be angry if you knew I had allowed Maritza out of my sight and so I hid until you had gone. That was when Vasily and his friend came along. I think, but I'm not sure, that he had just given him some money.'

'I've no doubt of it,' came the grim reply. 'So you put two and two together when you found the men had disappeared from the ballroom, eh? No wonder our friend thought we were accomplices when he came upon you lingering near the doorway of our meeting place,' Michael murmured, but to her irritation he did not elaborate further. 'The man was known to me, by the way. A Holsteiner—a paid assassin. Only before tonight I could never prove it.'

'How—how horrible! Then I was right—Vasily was trying to make you angry enough to follow him blindly . . .'

'Without a second thought,' Michael replied with a nod. 'Anger can very effectively blind all the senses, and make a cautious man vulnerable. I sensed a trap, but how else could I react when Maritza was with him? He knows how much I love my sister and he used it to full advantage. I shall have to clip that young man's wings for good if he gives me any more trouble.'

'You—you knew he might make an attempt on your life?' Emma stammered. She was convinced now that the hatred the two men felt for each other had little or nothing to do with Maritza. With what then?

Michael lifted his shoulders and the movement brought a tightening of his lips.

'I see I shock you. This is not the first time, nor will it be the last, which is why I need someone to watch over Maritza.'

'In the future I will follow your orders to the letter,' Emma promised. 'I will never take sides again.' If only he would believe her!

'A dangerous pastime, taking sides.' His tone was thoughtful. He broke off, emitting a grunt of pain as he attempted to sit upright, but when Emma moved forward, hands outstretched to help him, they were brushed aside. 'Go to bed, mademoiselle, there is nothing more you can do for me. And I do not like being at a disadvantage.'

Disadvantage! As if he considered her someone who might want to harm him. An enemy! Whitefaced she stepped back, no sign of the pain his thoughtless words had inflicted visible either in her expression or in her voice as she answered quietly.

'As you wish, sir.'

Jan rushed to his master's side as she walked swiftly

from the room. She heard another stifled groan, but steeled herself not to look back, not to feel pity for the man who had just dismissed her. His pride would not allow him to accept her help. Was he remembering the night she had played nurse to his brother, and resenting the fact that she had once been concerned for him also?

In her room she dispensed with the services of the maid and wearily stripped off her ruined gown. After washing the grime from her hands and face, she climbed into bed, but sleep was now beyond her. She lay with the candles still alight, unable to close her eyes and try to sleep. Each attempt brought vividly to mind the sight of Michael falling to his knees, the memory of his blood on her hand. He had accepted that his life was in danger as an inevitable fact and she still could not comprehend why. Instead of rousing Maritza from her bed and giving her a good talking to, if not the hard flat of his hand across a tender spot, he had locked her in her room!

There had been no sound from within when Emma passed it. Either she had grown tired of her shouts being ignored or she was wise enough to realise how foolhardy it would be to anger her brother further. Emma did not envy her the next meeting with Michael.

A clock somewhere in the silent house struck two melancholy notes. Emma got up and slipped on a wrap, deciding to go down to the kitchen and make herself some hot chocolate in the hope it might induce the sleep she longed for. As her hand reached out for the door knob, it turned slowly. Alarmed she stepped back, but the next moment she gave a sigh of relief as the huge oak door swung noiselessly open on well-oiled hinges and Jan's face appeared in the opening.

In one hand he held a dwindling candle. The other was beckoning her urgently. Her heart leapt unsteadily. Something must be very wrong for him to seek her out at this hour.

'The Prince?' she whispered, and he nodded.

The fear mirrored in his expression was more explicit than any words. Belting her robe firmly around her waist, she motioned him to lead the way through the darkened corridors to his master's rooms on the floor above, bracing her mind against what she might find.

Her worst fears were realised when she discovered Michael outstretched across the bed—unconscious. The shoulder of his robe was soaked with bright red blood. He had been pretending his wound was less serious than it really was. Emma laid a trembling hand against his cheek. His skin burned beneath her touch, heralding the approach of a fever. He needed the expert care of a doctor—and she should send word to Nikolai.

'Jan, fetch the Prince's valet. He must be put to bed immediately, and then you will ride for the doctor as fast as you can,' she ordered.

Scarcely were the words uttered than she heard the sound of the door being securely locked and spun around to see Jan standing with his back against it.

'Have you taken leave of your senses? Unlock that at once and do as you are told. Your master's life could very well depend on it.'

The lad gave a stubborn shake of his head and when she started towards him, he half-drew the knife in his belt, the same weapon he had used to kill the Holsteiner paid to murder Michael.

'Jan, for pity's sake . . . why are you doing this? Don't you understand I need help? I cannot undress the Prince, and he is feverish—someone will have to stay with him for the rest of tonight.'

What was it she did not know? Emma's thoughts were in a turmoil. Jan loved his master too much deliberately to endanger his life. He could only be acting on orders given to him before Michael passed out—implicit instructions he was determined not to disobey under any circumstances. She would have to manage alone.

'Help me with his clothes, then you will have to do the rest.' Emma's sharp tone hid the apprehension mounting inside her at the sight of Michael's terrible colour as she turned him over and proceeded to pull off his dressing-gown. Now he was helpless—at the disadvantage he despised. Had he sent Jan to fetch her, or had the boy acted on his own once he realised the seriousness of the situation? She glared at Jan who moved slowly to the bedside but made no attempt to help her, until she looked up at him appealingly. Slowly his hand fell away from the knife and he leaned forward to pull off Michael's boots.

Together they managed to ease away the blood-soaked shirt. A great sickness rose inside Emma as she found the saturated piece of cloth he had placed against the wound which was now bleeding freely again. She turned to one side, indicating Jan should finish the undressing.

In the adjoining dressing-room, she found a jug of water and towels and a cupboard full of fresh linen. She tore one of the linen sheets into long strips to use as bandages. When she went back, Jan was pulling the covers over Michael's unconscious form with the loving care of a mother tending a young child, she thought. She set down the things she held on a small table and moved closer to the bed.

'I need more light—and something to prevent the wound from becoming infected. Some vodka—or spirits of some kind . . .'

Jan made no sound as he crossed the floor, bringing first another three candles and then an earthenware jug taken from a chest at the foot of the bed, but she knew he was watching her every movement.

'Tear this into two pieces and soak one in whatever is in that jug,' she said, motioning to a towel.

After she had cleaned the wound, he helped her to lift the injured man sufficiently to place the soaked pad around his shoulder, binding it in place with strips of sheet. Michael had been right in his assumption that the wound was not serious, inasmuch as the pistol ball had not smashed a bone, but he had lost a great deal of blood. That, together with the head injury, had brought about his collapse.

'There is nothing we can do now but wait and pray he

is strong enough to withstand the fever.' Emma sat up with a sigh. She had made a clumsy job of the bandaging, but with what she had to hand it was little wonder. She lightly touched Michael's forehead, now wet with sweat, and then moved slowly down over the muscular chest of dark hair until she felt the steady throb of life beneath her fingertips. A tired smile crept to her lips as Jan leaned forward, his young face betraying agitation for the first time since she had entered the room. 'You don't have to watch me any longer. I shall not leave his side.'

She did not care that the tears in her eyes might betray her secret, was unaware of the sudden dawning of realisation in his eyes as she turned her attention once more to her patient. All that mattered was Michael. Tomorrow, it would be different. She would be his sister's companion, his employee again. But tonight—although he would never know it—she was more. Much more!

She settled herself in a chair close to the bed—and within minutes her eyelids began to droop. Several times she dragged herself back from the realms of sleep, but the inevitable had to happen after the traumatic experience of the evening, and at last she could no longer stay awake.

The sound of a voice close by stirred her back into wakefulness. The urgency in it brought her bolt upright, her startled gaze sweeping the room, but nothing had changed. Jan lay outstretched across the doorway, a position he had taken up after ensuring that the stove would provide them with sufficient warmth through the night. He looked to be asleep, but she suspected otherwise.

A string of oaths came from the bed. She leapt up in alarm as Michael, with eyes wide with fever, struggled to sit up, and she threw herself down beside him.

'Be still! You must not struggle. You will begin bleeding again. Hush now, there is no-one here to harm you.'

Why did she say that, she wondered, as his muttering slowly subsided and she rearranged the covers over him. Who was there beside Vasily Zouroff who meant him bodily harm? She knew the answer now. Had Maritza not voiced her fears weeks ago, and Michael confirmed it himself tonight? Because of his close association with Catherine, he was in danger from the Czar's agents. She shuddered to think that Peter would someday rule Russia alone and unchallenged, having disposed, with the help of his Holstein soldiers, of all those who opposed him. His unwanted wife and children, soldiers like the Orloffs who were ready to give their lives for Catherine's cause, noble Princes from the royal houses who daily voiced their discontent like Nikolai Adashev—and Michael . . .

For a long while she sat on the edge of the bed, wiping his perspiring brow with a dampened cloth. They would never share such intimacy again.

The fingers which closed around hers, drawing them away from his forehead, were surprisingly strong. The pale eyes, opening suddenly, unexpectedly, on to her face were shadowed with great pain and had difficulty in focussing on the figure bending over him. Michael's gaze flickered to the door and then came back to her and the ghost of a smile eased the tautness of his lips.

'Michael Adashev protected by a boy and a chit of a girl . . . If I didn't hurt so I would laugh. How long have I been like this?'

The undercurrent of mockery in his tone momentarily robbed Emma of an answer. Here she was thinking he was almost at death's door, and now he seemed in full possession of his faculties. Either he had the constitution of a horse or this was only a brief return to consciousness before the full force of the fever devastated his body and mind.

'You do not seem to be as badly hurt as I thought, Sir. Obviously you have no further need of me. If you will release me I will return to the comfort of my bed.'

'And deprive me of the gentle touch of your fingers against my burning brow?' Her indignation only served to increase his apparent amusement.

'I am sure Jan is as competent to provide you with that

service,' she returned sharply. 'If not him—then one of the other servants . . .'

'He has already disobeyed me by bringing you here . . . Did you come out of the goodness of your heart?' Michael interrupted. 'Damn it, I feel as weak as a new-born colt. Bring me a drink, there's a good girl. Vodka—not water.'

Reluctantly Emma did as he ordered and held the goblet against his lips while he drank. She did not approve of him taking strong drink in his condition, but something about his manner told her that it would be unwise to argue. He turned his head and explored the bandages swathed about his shoulder.

'I am in your debt.' His mood changed abruptly. The mockery vanished.

'Not at all. Jan gave me little choice. The moment I entered the room he locked the door and refused to allow me to leave again, and he made it quite plain he would use that knife of his if I tried.'

'He will answer to me for involving you against my wishes, but at this very moment I must admit to feeling glad he disobeyed me. I was in no condition to help myself. You do not understand my motives for wanting to keep what has happened tonight a secret?'

'Yes, I think I do. Apart from wanting to protect Maritza's reputation, I believe you also fear another assassination attempt. And not from Vasily Zouroff the next time.'

'Fear is not the word I would use—guard against, perhaps, is more apt.' Michael's voice was barely audible and she was alarmed to see beads of sweat gathering again on his brow. As she wiped them away with a clean towel, he gave a crooked grin.

'You will make some fortunate man a good and faithful wife, my little English miss. There were many men who found you attractive tonight, do you know that? How would you like a rich husband . . . ?'

'You—you cannot be serious,' she gasped.

'Why not? Did you not tell me, once, you would never

marry for love, as your mother did, that you would settle only for security. Tell me what you really want out of life and you shall have it. I will find you the most eligible bachelor in Petersburg if you can truthfully tell me that will make you happy.'

'It will not,' Emma declared, bright colour staining her cheeks. It had to be the fever making him talk this way.

'Marry for money only then. Perhaps you will find what you seek in fine clothes, jewels, a title perhaps . . .'

'What have such things brought to Anne? She is desperately unhappy.' The words slipped out without forethought.

'With good reason. Or do you still deny Nikolai's interest in you.'

'I have already told you the truth, but you choose to believe otherwise.'

'I believe the evidence of my own eyes. Have you not met in secret?'

'Yes, but not the way you mean . . . it was not planned.' Emma's head was throbbing with the fight against tiredness.

'Were you not holding hands when I came upon you?' The questions were being flung at her. A wild look had crept into Michael's pale eyes; they glittered in the candlelight, never leaving her face for an instant. She sensed some enormous agitation raging inside him, incensed by the throes of fever.

'No. Nikolai was holding my hand . . . there is a difference . . .' Again she was not allowed to finish.

'And his kiss? Tell me, did you enjoy that?'

'It was a peck on the cheek . . . the kind a brother would have given me.'

'Somehow I do not think you look on him as your brother, but whether he made the first move, or you, it is unimportant now. You will not be alone with him again. Do I make myself understood?'

She would agree to anything to make him lie back and rest and nodded vigorously. The movement brought the soft cloud of black hair swirling about her shoulders.

'I am thirsty . . .'

As she leaned towards the table to reach the goblet of vodka, Emma found herself suddenly seized and drawn down against his chest. The way he was having to fight for breath told her that his anger was taking a swift toll of his limited strength. It was probable she could free herself if she tried, but in doing so she might reopen his wound. The look in his eyes frightened her, yet somehow she managed to conquer her fear and remained still in his grasp.

'I could put my brand on you now—this minute. And I swear you would enjoy it. More so than with my brother . . .'

The inference behind the words shocked her even more than the threat. He was too weak to do her any real harm, yet some madness in him was driving him on to scorn and wound her. 'Don't look so terrified. Unwilling women are not to my taste—although I am not so sure you would be a reluctant participant.'

'First you accuse me of making eyes at Nikolai. Now you suggest I—I would . . . Your insinuation is unforgivable. He is a friend—nothing more. Why won't you believe me?'

'You try as forcefully to convince me of that as you do that we are and always will be enemies. But you know that is not true. Adversaries perhaps, but not enemies. We are too much alike.' Michael's lips brushed her cheek, burned her skin for a brief moment before she twisted her head away. 'When I hold a woman, kiss her, she knows exactly what my intentions are . . .' He caught her chin in his thumb and forefinger, dragging her mouth down to his. She did not resist—dared not. She wanted his arms about her, had dreamed of his kisses, but not like this! Not as if he hated her! 'You see, I can give you what Nikolai was willing to give . . . more . . . and I have no wife . . .'

'Even when you are wed, what will that matter? Your poor wife will not be able to command your presence like the Czarina does.' Emma's scornful tones were as effective as a slap across his face. She was thrust back from him.

'That is twice you have inferred we share a relationship. Be careful, my little viper-tongue, you are in no position to spit fire at me. Do you need reminding I am not only your employer, but your lord and master if I so choose. You can go nowhere, do nothing without my consent. I have allowed you the freedom you desired because I admired your spirit, your determination to rise above the humiliation Anne's parents forced you to endure, but I can deprive you of it just as easily. Beware you do not arouse the devil in me again. You will find me harder to handle than Nikolai . . .'

'Oh—oh, you are insufferable!' Hot tears scalded Emma's cheeks. He flinched as one fell onto the pillow beside him and slowly his hands fell away from her wrists, the wildness died out of his expression. For a long moment he simply stared at her, as if seeing her for the first time. Then his eyes closed and only the sound of his laboured breathing broke the silence of the room.

How long she sat shivering at his side Emma did not know. She was shaken to the core, unable to believe the slanderous accusations and threats Michael had uttered. He had been like a man possessed—but possessed by what?

Jan appeared to have slept through the whole incredible conversation, but she doubted it. His devotion to his master would prevent him from trusting her completely. Those alert eyes would have seen everything—the sharp ears caught every whispered insult.

For the next hour Michael tossed and turned restlessly under her watchful gaze. When sleep threatened to overwhelm her she paced the floor until the urge to sit down and relinquish her vigil had vanished. She was beginning to think he might be growing calmer when he began to roll his head on the pillows, muttering incoherently. She watched his hands bunch into tight fists time and time again as if he was in the grip of a nightmare. She returned to his side to try and calm him, forcing his fingers apart and lacing her own through them, holding them fast. She had not prayed in many years, not since the death of her mother had left her feeling bitter and deprived of love, of faith, but her lips moved in silent prayer now, her eyes locked on the icon of the Virgin in the alcove above the bed.

'No-one must know,' Michael groaned. 'No-one . . . promise me . . .'

'You have my word,' Emma replied through quivering lips. She did not even know if he understood her.

'I must not be seen like this . . . keep everyone away . . .'

'Jan is guarding the door. You are safe.'

'Stay with me . . . don't leave . . .' His fingers curled possessively over hers. Under any other circumstances, Emma thought, fighting back the tears . . .

His breathing grew easier, deeper, and she knew the crisis she had dreaded had passed. The first grey light of dawn was creeping through the window as she surrendered to the urge to sleep.

Emma was aroused by a thunderous knocking on the door. Loud and insistent though it was it took her several minutes to remember where she was. She had fallen asleep, still holding tightly to Michael's hands which were now cool to the touch. The fever had left him and he was sleeping peacefully, although it would not be for much longer if she did not silence whoever was outside. Bright sunlight was filling the room, indicating it was well into morning.

'Michael. Why the devil is this door locked?'

Nikolai's voice! Emma winced as she pulled herself upright, straightening cramped limbs. From the doorway Jan looked at her questioningly. She had promised that no-one should see Michael in his present state, but if she did not admit Nikolai he might very well break the door down from the sound of it. And if she could trust anyone it would surely be him.

'Open it,' she ordered, 'but admit only Prince Nikolai.'

She turned away, quickly smoothing some of the creases from her wrap and trying to bring some order to her hair. What a mess she looked. Whatever would people think if they saw her now?

The moment Jan began to ease the door open, Nikolai put his booted foot behind it and thrust it wide open, giving the curious servants clustered outside in the corridor a clear view of the startled English girl in night attire—and the sleeping Michael. The looks they exchanged told Emma they believed she had spent the night in the room for a far different purpose.

Jan slammed the door in their faces and gesticulated wildly with his hands, but Nikolai shook his head.

'You know I don't understand you, boy.' He did not seem in any way perturbed at Emma's presence in his brother's room and brought a flush of embarrassed colour to her cheeks by commenting with an almost wicked grin: 'My apologies, little cousin. I have never known Michael to lock his door before. I should have realised he was—otherwise occupied.'

'There has been an accident—last night, on the way back from Mon Plaisir,' she began. How much should she tell him?

'Accident be damned,' a weak voice declared from the bed, saving her further explanation. 'Zouroff sent an assassin after me. He almost killed us both—would have if Jan hadn't dealt with him. Help me up, someone—I'm devilish thirsty and my head feels as if it has been split in two.'

Emma started forward, but Nikolai was ahead of her, lifting Michael into a sitting position. She could have wept with relief. Her prayers had been answered.

'Good God, man, you need a doctor,' Nikolai ejaculated, seeing the thick bandages for the first time. His face went almost as grey as his brother's.

'No. I have been well cared for, although from what I can remember, I don't think I deserved it,' Michael returned, gingerly touching the wound at his temple, and his gaze flickered across to where Emma stood.

'I will have some hot broth sent up from the kitchen. I think you should be able to manage that. And—and then I must go and dress . . .' she faltered. She could not escape quickly enough from the intent gaze of those pale eyes. She had hoped the fever would have wiped his memory clean of what had passed between them.

'I was not on my best behaviour—that I recall,' Michael murmured. 'You did not deserve the things I said to you . . .'

'It was the fever talking, sir. I took no notice whatsoever,' she lied and was aware of a frown growing on Nikolai's face.

Emma was tired and her nerves were frayed to breaking point. The sight of two giggling maids lingering outside the door snapped the last of her self-control and she ran all the way back to her room, not caring who saw her undignified exit, so long as she reached the sanctuary of it before the tears came.

CHAPTER NINE

EMMA stood in the doorway of her bedroom, staring across at the tall, slender woman who turned from the window at her entrance and looked at her in wide-eyed surprise. Of all people, her cousin Anne was the last person she wanted to see. After Michael's outburst, still vivid in her mind, if anyone so much as hinted she was interested in Nikolai, she would scream.

'Good heavens, Emma. You look as if you have been dragged through a hedge backwards,' Anne declared. 'Where have you been? Why was your bed not slept in? And what is this I hear about Michael being injured last night? Someone said the carriage overturned.'

'Anne, please—no questions,' Emma pleaded, reeling unsteadily towards a chair. 'I am very tired.'

'Have you been up all night? Yes, I can see you have, and I've no need to ask where. I heard one of the servants gossiping on my way up here. Needless to say I soundly boxed the girl's ears. The very idea! Insinuating you—and Michael . . .!'

Emma raised a tear-streaked face to look at her cousin and, after a moment, said in a stifled tone:

'You were quick enough to accuse me of an association with Nikolai when we were only talking together.'

To her amazement Anne dropped to her knees beside the chair, her expression contrite. Sunlight glinted on the ringed hand she laid on Emma's arm. The change in her since they had last met was quite remarkable, Emma thought. She looked almost—radiant!

'Will you ever forgive my stupidity? I was jealous—I admit it. I can now. Oh, Emma, say we are friends again. I am so happy. I want you to share it with me. I am selfish, and petty, and spoilt—everything you have said I am, but I am going to change, I have promised Nikolai . . .'

'Has—has something happened between you?'

'He loves me—he truly does, and I believe him now. I love him too, you see, but you already guessed that, didn't you? I have never been able to hide anything from you, even when we were children.' Anne sat back on her heels, her eyes bright with excitement. Tired as she was, Emma felt as if a great weight had been lifted from her shoulders. 'What a man I have married,' Anne sighed. 'Until yesterday I never realised it. He—he refused to go to the ball, or to let me go either. He was furious over the way I had acted towards you in the garden and he told me so in no uncertain terms. I wanted to see Michael last night, to make him send you away, but Nikolai refused to allow me to leave the house. He said Michael was taking you and Maritza to Mon Plaisir and you were to be presented formally to the Czarina—that it was your special night and I was not going to spoil it for you. We had a terrible argument. Do you know what he did?' Her voice dropped to a whisper. 'He—he pulled me over his knee like—like a naughty little child, and spanked me. Not even papa has ever dared do such a thing. Oh, Emma, I never knew I could hurt so much! And then he told me . . . everything . . .'

'Wait—wait,' Emma cried, 'my mind is reeling. Do you mean Nikolai deliberately kept you at Belmaya as—as a kind of punishment?' Shades of Michael, she thought, staring at her cousin in disbelief.

'There was one moment when I thought he meant to strike me. Am I forgiven?' Anne pleaded and the sincerity in her tone told Emma that she really wanted the rift between them to be healed. She gave a faint nod.

With a squeal of delight, which did not go with the elegant figure she presented in a beautiful dress of peach satin, Anne threw her arms around Emma and hugged her.

'I will never be horrid to you again—or to mama or

papa. Nikolai has promised they may stay in the house in Petersburg as long as they wish. Will that not be wonderful?'

'I am very pleased they are able to come. It will be an exciting trip for them,' Emma admitted, smothering a yawn.

'Oh, my poor dear, you are exhausted,' Anne said, jumping to her feet. 'Have you eaten? No, of course not . . . you have been with Michael all night. You must have some food, but first a bath to revive you.'

Emma could scarcely believe her ears or her eyes as Anne summoned her maid, ordered a hot bath to be prepared and breakfast sent up within half-an-hour. She had never before shown her cousin such consideration. Everything about her manner proclaimed a drastic change had taken place. Michael would be relieved the marriage had begun to work at last, but how would he react to the news of the Tarrants' arrival, contrary to his wishes?

The hot water scented with pungent rose petal essence soothed the tiredness from Emma's body. She leaned her head against the back of the porcelain tub and stared across at Anne who was relaxing in a nearby chair. She positively glowed with happiness.

'You have told Nikolai how you feel towards him, of course,' she said.

'While we were arguing he was quite horrid to me, but afterwards he held me in his arms and told me what a silly goose I was to think he would ever love another woman. I couldn't help myself, Emma. It was as if I had never really known him. I can make him happy—I know it.'

'I am sure of it,' Emma replied and she meant it.

'How did it come about you were with Michael all last night?' Anne asked, giving her a curious look. 'I should have expected Maritza to show more concern for her brother. And surely one of the servants could have sat with him?'

'Maritza was rather—indiscreet last night. She went

off on her own with a young man. Consequently she has been confined to her room.' Emma thought it wiser to omit a few of the more important facts.

'Not Vasily Zouroff? I met him a few weeks ago. Rather a forward young man, I thought, with his eye more on Maritza's dowry than anything else. Michael dislikes him intensely,' Anne said, helping herself to several grapes from the well-laden breakfast table set up in the middle of the room. She cast another, more speculative, look into Emma's face as they sat down some minutes later. 'So you were alone with him all night. No wonder the whole place is buzzing this morning.'

'You don't understand,' Emma protested. 'There was no-one else. Besides, we were not alone. Jan, Prince Michael's body servant, was in the room.'

'I think I understand only too well, my girl. You gave yourself away with those tears earlier. You have fallen in love with the arrogant brute, haven't you?'

'He—he isn't a brute,' Emma blurted out, and then gave a miserable nod. 'You must say nothing. I could not stay here if he found out.'

'And you are content—just to be here with him,' Anne murmured. 'I would not be able to bear it.'

'What choice do I have?'

'You know of course he is in love with someone else? Or rather infatuated is a better description. I heard him talking to Nikolai once. From what he said it seems this woman hasn't looked twice in his direction and is totally unaware of how he feels towards her . . .' she broke off as Emma went pale. 'Forgive me, but isn't it better you know? He will use you if you allow it, until such time as she realises his feelings. I doubt if she will refuse the chance of marrying a Prince of the House of Adashev, whoever she is.'

Emma picked at the food on her plate. Suddenly her appetite had gone. She knew Michael had already chosen a wife; he had told her so himself, but not until Anne brought it out into the open did she fully realise the hopelessness of her position, the heartbreak her decision to stay would bring her.

'Last night he needed me,' she replied slowly. 'Perhaps he will again. I could be content with that.'

'You deserve better . . . a man of your own to care for you.'

'Maritza wants to find me a husband.'

'Then let her. Think of yourself, as I have for so many years. I used you abominably, Emma. Our friendship I despised because you were always in control of yourself, while I went to pieces whenever a crisis arose. I avoided the ties of our blood relationship because deep in my heart I always admired your mother—envied her the love she found; love she refused to give up or deny even at the cost of cutting herself off from her own family. I even came to despise the way my own parents took advantage of her pitiful condition after Culloden. They were unfair to you both. Most of all—I was unfair . . .'

'Don't, Anne, please. Let it all be in the past. If you go on I shall start to weep again.' Emma smiled at her through a mist of tears. 'Thank you for confiding in me—for allowing me to share your happiness . . .'

'If only there was something I could do for you.'

'Michael is not badly hurt. At the moment that is all that matters just now.'

'One day you may find you want more,' Anne said as she rose to her feet. 'Goodness, is that the time? Nikolai and I are going riding with the Kustovs this afternoon. Why don't you come with us? It will get you away from this house, and Michael, for a few hours. You could even stay overnight at Belmaya. Michael might begin to show some interest if you are not always at his beck and call.'

He had shown interest, Emma mused, as they went downstairs, a disturbing amount, of late.

Nikolai came out of the study as they passed, pushing a sheaf of papers into an inside pocket. A smile lit up his features as he saw them together and talking amiably.

'You have done as I asked?' he murmured, taking his wife by the arm.

'Have I not promised to be an obedient wife?' Anne laughed softly, pursing her lips. 'I have made my peace with Emma. We shall never quarrel again.'

'Then I am well pleased.' Nikolai's gaze rested thoughtfully on Emma's still pale cheeks. What had passed between him and his brother after she had left, she wondered. His expression gave nothing away. 'And you, little cousin, have my undying gratitude for last night's work.'

'I did nothing . . .'

'That is a matter of opinion. Michael is not taken to exaggeration. I believe what he has told me and I will not forget it.'

'Come to tea on Thursday and bring Maritza,' Anne suggested.

'We shall be in Petersburg on Tuesday, my love,' Nikolai answered. 'Michael and I have just been working out the details. We shall all travel together and have the house prepared for the arrival of your parents.'

'St Petersburg—so soon! Oh, Nikolai, how wonderful! Will they meet all our friends? Do you think you could persuade Michael to present them to the Czarina? How mama would love that.'

As Anne herself would have done once, Emma thought, as she stood in the doorway, waving to them both until the carriage disappeared from sight around a bend in the drive. She certainly had changed. How marvellous love could be for some people.

'Emma.' She was almost at the staircase when the sound of Michael's voice from behind halted her. With wildly beating heart she turned and saw him standing fully dressed in the study. How pleasant he made her name sound!

'What are you doing out of bed? You should be resting.' Was he mad to get up so soon? All those long hours of nursing would be to no avail if the fever returned to weken him further.

'Please come in here for a moment. I would prefer what I have to say to be for your ears only.'

Emma had forgotten the servants. She hurried past him, ignoring the amused gleam in the eye of the footman who closed the door after them.

'I am sorry . . . I did not think,' she began lamely, but he waved aside the apology.

'Recently it seems I am the one who has not been thinking clearly,' Michael said meaningly. His left arm was carefully supported in a black silk scarf tied around his neck and his features were grey and drawn. The injuries he had sustained would have kept a lesser man confined to bed, she thought. 'Sit down, you look tired and I am in no condition to stand for long, despite your excellent ministering.'

As she perched herself on the edge of a chair, he relaxed with a deep sigh into a huge leather armchair before the fireplace.

'That's better. Have you eaten?' He motioned to the tray containing food and a samovar of coffee on the table at his side.

'Yes—with Anne.'

'Ah, yes—your cousin. No more worries in that direction, thank God. She apologised for her unpleasant attitude of the last few weeks, I hope?'

'Yes, although it was not necessary. Not really. In her place I might very well have acted the same way. She loves Nikolai, you see . . .'

'So he tells me. My brother is full of surprises this morning. That is not all I learned . . .' His tone and the narrowing of those blue eyes indicated he knew the truth. She waited for the explosion to come, yet nothing happened. No recriminations, no outbursts of temper—nothing. At last she could stand his silence no longer.

'I know I went against your explicit instructions, but it was for the best,' she cried. 'Not only was Anne unhappy, but Nikolai too. Their marriage has a chance of survival now . . .'

'So you are concerned for my brother after all,' came the swift retort and she realised that his tortuous silence had been deliberate—to draw her out and force an explanation.

'As a friend. Since the first moment I arrived in Russia he has been kind to me. I value his friendship.' There, it was said. Let him think what he liked!

'Would it were possible for me to possess such a staunch ally,' Michael returned with a cynical smile. 'I was wrong and I admit it. I allowed my concern for Nikolai to ride rough-shod over everything and everyone, as I fear I may well do when it comes to Maritza's future. I have the tendency to watch over those I love with the utmost dedication.'

'Your apology is accepted, sir.' The moment did not bring with it the satisfaction she had once expected. 'If that is all, may I go now? I am very tired.'

'And anxious to quit my presence as soon as possible. What a strange little creature you are. Stubborn the moment we are in disagreement—placid and rather shy the next. Have you no wish to enjoy your moment of triumph? Most women would. And you did say the day would come when I would be forced to make such a statement, did you not? Were you not waiting for it—anticipating it? No—I think not. You, I am fast discovering, are unlike any other woman I have ever encountered. Unfortunately, there is something about you which rouses the devil in me . . .' He broke off with a soft exclamation and, reaching into the pocket of his frilled shirt, brought out Emma's necklace and dangled it before her eyes. She had forgotten its existence in all the excitement. 'What do you propose I do with this? It's yours, you know. It was meant as a peace offering.'

'Maritza told me . . . I misunderstood,' Emma faltered. 'I thought . . .'

'That I intended to parade you before everyone at Mon Plaisir as a woman of—shall we say—easy virtue, open to accepting gifts in return for certain favours? We must like each other very much, my little Emma, to always be at each other's throats.' He tossed it onto the arm of her chair, but she made no move to take it.

'Like—I—?' The words stuck in Emma's throat. 'You are my employer . . .'

'And does that mean I cannot like you, or admire you, even seek your company?' Michael inquired.

He was being nice to her, Emma thought, as Anne had suspected he might, in an effort to alleviate the boredom of waiting for the woman he really loved to acknowledge at last his existence. When that happened she, Emma, would cease to be of interest to him. If only she was brave enough to seize what she suspected he was offering—to enjoy the stolen moments and have no regrets when the affair ended. Alas, she could not.

Michael rose to his feet and move closer to her chair. His nearness was unnerving. She could feel herself begin to tremble. She had trembled in his arms last night when his lips took possession of hers—and never wanted the moment to end! It must not happen again. She lowered her head, refusing to look at him, heard a note of annoyance creep into his tone as he demanded:

'Why do you find it so unbelievable that I find you interesting—stimulating?'

Only as an instrument with which to pass the days of uncertainty. Was the Czarina's attention now centred in another direction, forcing him to seek his pleasures elsewhere?

'You have already made it known to me that you have chosen a wife. Do the marriage vows you will take mean so little to you?' she challenged.

'When—and I repeat when—I make those vows, before God and my bride, they will be for life.'

'Then why . . . ?' She lifted her head and looked into his eyes and the sadness there made her quickly look away again.

'. . . do I speak to you this way? Come now, am I asking too much of you? Yes, perhaps I am . . . of one who has never known love, or the sleepless nights unrequited passion can bring. How could you understand? There are times when I fear the woman of my choice is not even aware I am on this earth. I have resigned myself to being patient, to wait until she realises what is in my heart and accepts it. But how time drags!'

'I think you love her very much.' As much as she loved him, would always love him despite this shattering declaration.

'You sound surprised. Do you think me incapable of the emotion?' Michael demanded in a startled tone. 'With both Nikolai and Maritza you have made it very clear I have behaved like some kind of devil by interfering in their lives. I gave my brother a wife who has brought him nothing but unhappiness . . .'

'That is past,' Emma broke in. Surely he did not doubt Anne's change of heart?

'I hope so, but there is still Maritza. You are wrong, you know. I am not as black-hearted as you believe, nor indifferent to the feelings of those around me, although I admit at times I find difficulty in communicating. In Maritza's eyes at this moment . . . well, I will not burden you with her explicit adjectives. In time she will—must, understand.' A heavy sigh escaped him. After a moment he turned to look out of the window which overlooked the stables. Emma felt a surge of alarm as she saw Jan leading out his black stallion.

'You are not going to ride him?' she asked in alarm.

'No, Jan will exercise him for me. Why do you show such concern for my welfare, yet shrink from any deeper involvement?' He half turned and stared at her quizzingly.

'It would not be seemly, sir, for us to share any relationship other than that of employer and employee.'

'Damn the English sense of propriety.' She winced at his harsh tone. 'All I ask is your friendship—no more than you shared with Nikolai. I'm not trying to get you into my bed, girl, pleasant though I'm sure the experience would be. I have need of someone I can trust. Have I not made that clear to you?'

'Friendship?' Emma was swept by conflicting reactions. Pleased—and yet if she was completely honest with herself—disappointed she could never share a deeper, more meaningful relationship with him. Yet, had she not accepted this is how it must be if she was to remain beneath his roof?

'How can you speak of trusting me when I allowed Maritza and Captain Zouroff to go off together?'

'Maritza has confirmed you were in no way responsible for what happened. I spoke to her while you were with your cousin. Zouroff told her you would be accompanying them, but then he drove off without you, making some excuse that you were dancing with a handsome young man and he did not have the heart to interrupt you. Maritza is young and impressionable . . . and she trusts him. His word would have been believed. She assures me he was a gentleman in every way,' Michael added dryly.

'With his hired man waiting to kill you I suppose he saw the advantages of continuing the charade,' Emma said. 'With you dead, Maritza would need someone to console her in her grief. Who better to turn to than the man she loves.'

She stared out across the flower gardens which stretched alongside the stables. She would miss this place terribly. It had been more of a home to her than the house in St Petersburg or even that of her aunt and uncle in London. But at least the busy social life would keep her mind occupied.

'Is Maritza to accompany us to St Petersburg?'

'And risk a full scale rebellion if I attempted to leave her behind? She knows I will tolerate no more clandestine meetings with Zouroff. She has not been told what really took place—will never know if I have my way. I shall take steps to ensure they are never alone together again and their meetings will be few and far between.'

'I fear she will try and disobey you,' Emma said, and he nodded gravely.

'So do I. Your expression tells me she has confided in you. No! Betray no secrets. I think I know what is on her mind.'

'As much as I sympathise with the way she feels just now, I agree that Vasily Zouroff is no good for her. I will do whatever I can to make her realise that.'

'And jeopardise what has grown between you?'

'A small thing to sacrifice with so much at stake.' For you both, she added silently.

Michael took one of her hands and touched it to his lips and then, turning it over, planted a kiss gently on the palm.

'No longer enemies, not even adversaries—now we are friends.'

When he did not let her go, Emma disengaged herself with a shaky laugh.

'Very well then, friends. As your friend, may I be allowed to advise you to rest for the remainder of the day.'

'I will stay here,' Michael said, returning to his chair. 'No-one will disturb me. You also must catch up on some sleep. Maritza will not require you today.'

As she closed the door quietly behind her Emma looked back at the figure already beginning to doze in the armchair. He offered friendship, not love, but she was grateful for even that small crumb.

The days before the household moved back to the city were hectic. Only for one brief evening did Emma notice Maritza to be in a subdued mood, and that was after she had been closeted with Michael in her sitting-room for over an hour. Both their voices had been heard raised in anger and then Michael had stormed out, leaving his sister in tears. Later Emma discovered he had threatened to make her live permanently at Malayevka the next time she disobeyed him, cut off from the soirées and parties and friends she loved so much.

He had apparently passed over his injuries lightly, attributing them to a badly aimed shot from a ragged-looking peasant who had attempted to rob the coach. Someone with a grudge, a man dismissed recently from the estates, he had said. The explanation had satisfied

Maritza whose primary concern was his threat to isolate her in the country.

'Vasily and I were very lucky not to have been stopped also,' she remarked as they took tea together out in the garden on the afternoon before leaving. 'Don't look so disapproving. Are you still angry at the trick he played on you? I shall make him apologise. It was very naughty of him to pretend you were dancing, but he wanted to be alone with me, Emma. I shall make him promise to be nice to you in the future.'

'I want no prompted apology, Maritza, and I do not think I would trust any of his promises. Surely he realised how provoking such an action was to your brother?' Emma returned, helping herself to a honey biscuit, the cook's speciality and her favourite at this time of the afternoon.

'Provoking! You sound as if he was deliberately trying to make Michael angry. Don't be silly, that is the last thing he wants to do. It is easy to see you have never been in love,' Maritza returned with a toss of her head. 'That was our first meeting in many months. How could he be natural with me in front of all those gaping people—friends of Michael's, like Alexei Orloff? That man has never liked Vasily and he is the worst gossip monger I know.'

'Has he reason?'

'Vasily came up through the ranks by sheer hard work and determination and dedication to duty. He did not have help like the Orloffs and others. They are jealous of him. He has told me even the Czarina has noticed him of late. If she should take an interest in him, then anything could happen. A promotion, a title. Michael could have no objections to our marriage then, could he?'

Emma was finding it increasingly difficult to understand how Vasily Zouroff, one of Catherine's guards, should have been on such friendly terms with a Holsteiner from the enemy camp of the Czar. The separation between the two was now very distinct. The thought had nagged away at her day and night until she was left with a very unpleasant conclusion. Was the young man prepared to further his ambitions by having a foot in both camps, being loyal to both parties concerned, until such time as he was forced to step to one side or the other and declare himself openly? She knew it was useless to try and question Maritza. The girl was totally infatuated and Emma dared not risk any rift in their friendship, for it was this which would enable her to stay close once they were back in St Petersburg.

As she entered the town house, followed by Anne and Nikolai who had accompanied them in a separate carriage, and by servants loaded with huge trunks and valises, Emma remembered the very first time she had set foot here, tired and disillusioned, a shadow of the girl who now climbed the stairs to her rooms in a pale blue travelling dress, her eyes bright with excitement.

No ante-chamber for her this time, nor was she to be relegated to some attic room, at the beck and call of her cousin. Her rooms adjoined those of Maritza's, small but comfortable, and when she stepped over the threshold it was to find her maid had already begun her unpacking.

Michael did not appear for the rest of the day. She had watched his face growing steadily greyer during the journey from Malayevka and knew his wound was taxing his still limited strength. She was not surprised when Nikolai informed them during the evening that he had decided to retire early. As they all sat together at dinner later, Emma felt a great sense of belonging steal over her—of being 'one of the family'. If only the shadow of Vasily Zouroff did not hover in the background, she thought, as Maritza's infectious giggle brought a smile to her lips. The girl was so happy . . .

The arrival of the Tarrants sent the whole household into a frenzy of activity. They were given the guest rooms on the second floor and Anne insisted on personally supervising all the arrangements, even down to the clean linen and bed-warmers. She had brought three of her own servants from Belmaya for the sole purpose of attending to the needs of her parents. Emma did not mind at all when her offer of help was refused, realising it was important for her cousin to become totally involved. In making them so welcome perhaps she was trying to atone for some of the years of anxiety she had caused them with her thoughtless spendthrift ways which had so drained their resources.

Small gifts appeared unexpectedly on Emma's dressing table: perfume, or an item of jewellery, even clothes, not unwanted cast-offs as in the past, but items of value like a beautiful woollen cloak lined with white fur, and the most exquisite lace-trimmed nightgown created from material so flimsy it made Emma blush when she held it against her. Emma suspected Anne was also trying to atone to her.

Emma was out shopping with Maritza when the Tarrants arrived. Hearing the sound of happy, excited voices coming from their rooms as she passed, she decided to leave her reunion with them until that evening.

What would they think of her now, she wondered, as she dressed for dinner. No longer a servant as she had been in their household, but holding a position of importance in one of the most influential families in Russia. They must surely be proud of her advancement. It would be nice if the feeling of belonging she was experiencing extended to include her mother's family, with whom she had always considered herself an outsider, a liability, unwanted and unloved.

For more formal gatherings, Emma's hair was always dressed and curled, but when dinner was *en famille* she had begun to leave it loose, sweeping the thick tresses back from her face with combs or ribbons. Tonight she secured it with a scarlet bow. Matching satin ribbons slashed the sleeves and skirt of her white gown, only finished that day with the help of one of the sewing maids. She had intended to keep it for her first ball in St Petersburg, but had decided that tonight was, in itself, a grand occasion and that she should look her best.

No expense had been spared for the Tarrants' first night in the city. The cook, with whom Emma was on excellent terms, had told her earlier of the delicious, mouth-watering pâtés and smoked hams purchased from shops in the German quarter, the light, fragrant wines from the French, not to mention the abundance of roasted wild pheasant and chickens cooked in wines, the pastries and after-dinner delicacies she herself had been preparing all day. And Prince Michael had brought a dozen bottles of vintage brandy from his private cellar at Malayevka—an honour indeed for the English visitors! The cook's tone told Emma such a thing had never happened before. An honour indeed, since he had not wanted the visitors in the first place, she thought.

She was standing by the windows of the sitting-room, looking out towards the bleak shape of the Winter Palace outlined against the redness of a dying sunset, when there came a quiet knock on the door. Not until a louder, more insistent knock came did she realise she had sent her maid away.

'Come in.'

The sight of the tall figure who entered made her heart leap unexpectedly with pleasure. Michael wore a dark green coat and breeches, embroidered with gold thread. A huge, brilliant white diamond flashed in the lace jabot at his throat. She noticed he was still pale, but perhaps it was only because she cared so deeply that she was aware of it and the shadowing beneath the pale eyes which swept across the room to where she stood. He had discarded the scarf supporting his injured arm. To avoid awkward questions, she suspected.

'I thought perhaps you had already gone downstairs.' He advanced to her side and glanced out of the window before turning to face her, his expression quizzical.

'I was daydreaming,' she confessed.

'Not thinking of Malayevka already? We have been here less than a week.' His tone was light, but she felt he would have preferred to have been in the country still, with his beloved house, his horses and his solitude. 'Lord and Lady Tarrant are already in the drawing-room with Nikolai,' he said. 'I suspect your cousin is making herself look radiant, and for once I shall forgive her a late appearance. I did not realise she was so close to them. The impression they gave me when we met . . . No matter; the two families are reunited. Perhaps it is for the best.'

Emma was conscious of his gaze inspecting her appearance. In the mirror behind him she could sce her reflection. The cloud of black hair about her shoulders made her look younger than her nineteen years and she was startled to notice she had lost weight considerably during the months in the country. Too many long walks and energetic rides on horseback. She looked positively thin!

'Will you refuse to take this back if I offer it to you again?' Michael asked, and she saw he was holding out to her the diamond and ruby necklace.

'Will—will it displease you if I do?' How could she accept such a gift? And yet she wanted to with all her heart.

'Now that you know it is offered in friendship? Yes, it would.'

Without a word she lifted her hair aside and allowed him to fasten it around her neck, hoping he did not see the pleasure which leapt to her eyes at his sincere answer.

'Am I forgiven now?' Michael asked.

'Forgiven, sir? For what?' That moment in his bedroom when he had held her in his arms and kissed her—wanted her? Or for forcing her to choose between friendship with his sister and her loyalty to the House of Adashev—to him?

'For whatever made you sad before we left Malayevka.'

'I could not be happier.' Was it possible he did not really remember?

'Then why do your eyes tell me a different story?'

'Perhaps you have mistaken my apprehension at meeting my aunt and uncle again after all this time as sadness,' she lied, with quickening heartbeats.

'Then we must dispel any fears at once,' came the firm reply as he tucked her arm beneath his and guided her to the door.

As Emma entered the drawing-room with Michael at her side, she sensed the sudden incredulity which surfaced in the Tarrants as they recognised her. Surprise, then bewilderment, registered in their faces as their eyes took in her dress, the necklace at her throat, the high-heeled satin shoes peeping beneath the hem of her underskirts. Then, with a soft cry, Elizabeth Tarrant left her husband to greet her niece with hugs and kisses, the like of which Emma had never experienced before. She stood in an embarrassed silence in the arms of her aunt.

'My dear, you look quite charming—and so like your dear mother. I was saying to George only the other day how like her you had grown. Why, it is almost as if you were sisters.' Then, without giving her a chance to answer, 'I trust she has given no cause for complaint, Prince Michael? She always was rather head-strong. All that Scots blood, you know. But with firm handling . . .'

'On the contrary, my family have taken her to their hearts,' Michael answered, and Anne hurried forward at the tightening of his lips, to lead her mother back to the sofa.

'Mama, don't fuss so. Things have changed since Emma and I first arrived in Russia. She has been introduced to the Czarina Catherine herself, and is now Maritza's companion. I did tell you this afternoon, if you remember.'

'After the exhausting journey your mama was in no condition to listen to your chatter,' George Tarrant returned, a trifle dryly. He was also embarrassed at the meeting, Emma thought.

Did he see her mother in her too? Was he remembering the terrible life he had imposed on her in order to protect his precious name? Did he regret the harsh words and humiliation he had forced her to endure?

'I am pleased to see you again, uncle. I hope you are well.' Emma curtsied politely. She could not bring herself to offer a warmer greeting. Not yet, at least—and she had thought it would be so easy.

The carefree atmosphere at the dinner table relaxed her and she began to regret the momentary remembrance of the past which had prevented her from welcoming the Tarrants as she had planned. Perhaps, in time, when they could look at her and not be disturbed by the likeness she held to her mother, she could think of past events without bitterness.

Anne, whose tongue had not been still since they sat down, suddenly lapsed into silence. Emma watched her cousin put down her silver fork and steal an almost shy glance at the husband at her side. A smile crossed Nikolai's face. His hand covered hers as he said softly:

'Tell them.'

'May I? You don't mind?'

'That your parents and my own brother and sister should learn tonight that I am the happiest man in Christendom? Tell them.'

'I am *enceinte*,' Anne whispered, two bright spots of colour appearing in her cheeks. 'I am to have a child.'

'A son, an heir to Belmaya,' Nikolai added.

As congratulations flowed across the table, Emma's eyes were on Michael. He beckoned a servant to fill their glasses to the brim, and then rose to offer a toast to the heir. Nothing in his voice or in his expression betrayed what Emma suspected he was thinking. His thoughts at that moment, too, must surely be dwelling on the son he would have—the day he would proudly make the same announcement. An heir for Malayevka—a son for Michael Adashev!

'You will wish to remain in Petersburg until after the child is born, of course,' he said to the Tarrants, resuming his seat.

'Could they, Michael?' Anne seized on the suggestion eagerly. 'Or they could stay at Belmaya with us.'

'And deprive them of all the outings I know you are planning? Surely you are not retiring to the country again so soon. She is not unwell is she, Nikolai?'

'Of course not,' his brother returned, 'but we have discussed it and we thought—well, it would be easier, would it not?'

'Nonsense, I will not hear of it. We will find them a house in the vicinity and they shall stay as long as they wish. Who knows, they may even decide to make Russia their home too.'

'Michael, you are too generous,' Anne breathed. She was as taken aback with the idea as Emma. This was the man she had accused of being inhuman and cruel—oblivious to her needs, her happiness!

'Your happiness, and that of my brother, is my prime concern. You should know that by now,' Michael replied with a slow smile. 'Shall we adjourn to the drawing-room? I have some excellent brandy there demanding appreciation.'

'Has your cousin's news pleased you?' Michael lingered behind to wait for Emma.

'Very much. I am pleased for them both.'

'Anne has taken it better than I expected. She is already planning the nursery. To have her parents with her will mean a great deal. Nikolai has just told me why he decided to tak the Tarrants to Belmaya. It appears he thought I was still angry at the deception the two of you played on me. How foolish of him even to consider such a thing. I have been looking after his interests ever since we were children. There is nothing I would not do for him. I used to take his part against our father, I remember. He was not strong, you understand—some illness when he was five years old. He could not play games with other children, and during the winter months he rarely ventured outdoors. It was a miserable existence. Had it not been for our mother, his life would have been unbearable. But I am boring you.'

'No,' Emma protested softly. 'Please go on.'

'You have no brothers or sisters, no family except the

Tarrants, with whom you were not happy,' Michael continued. 'That is a pity. It is not good to be alone. I would like to think you are settled with us.'

'So long as you are satisfied with me, sir, then I am well content.'

Michael threw her an odd look, as if he had expected his question to produce a different answer. In the drawing-room she looked past him to where Nikolai sat on the arm of his wife's chair, one arm around her shoulders.

'They are well matched after all,' she said. 'You recognised in Anne a strength of character even I did not realise she possessed, but if you were so sure of her, why did you find it necessary to meet us at the inn and pretend to be one of your own servants?' It was a question she could no longer contain.

A smile deepened the corners of Michael's mouth.

'I came to inspect the prospective bride, what else? I wanted to be sure of the choice I had made before it was too late. I thought France might have changed the girl I had first seen at court.'

France—where Emma had worn that yellow dress and he had remembered the brief moment long enough to select one similar for her to wear to her cousin's wedding! What a complex character he was! She would never fully understand what motivated his often unpredictable actions.

Many times during that evening as she sat with the others, her fingers strayed to the necklace at her throat. A gift given in friendship. She would never have a more staunch ally in times of need—nor so daunting an adversary.

Friendship was not love, but she had never been more happy in all her young life.

CHAPTER TEN

JUNE in St Petersburg was an extravaganza of parties which invariably went on until dawn, endless lunches with Maritza and her friends. Watchful, ever watchful for the slightest attempt to meet secretly the man she loved, Emma found her behaviour impeccable. She was so well behaved, that Emma became doubly suspicious of her actions.

On rare occasions Michael accompanied them to the theatre or to the opera, but often, Emma noticed, he was absent from the house for most of the night. More than once as she was climbing into bed in the early hours, she heard him return, and she listened to him pass her room on the way upstairs, before she closed her eyes and tried to close her mind to the thought of him with Catherine.

No longer was there any doubt in her mind that not only the Czarina, but anyone loyal to her, was in danger. Several of her immediate followers had been unexpectedly snatched from their homes by the Czar's guards and confined in the fortress of St Peter and St Paul. Now Peter was threatening to arrest his wife and confine her in the prison of Schlusselburg, something with which he himself had often been threatened by the late Empress Elizabeth when he disobeyed her. Only the intervention of his uncle by marriage, Prince George of Holstein, of whom he was very fond, prevented him from implementing the drastic move, which in itself would have been enough to cause an uprising in the army.

While the Orloff brothers, now that Alexei had been appointed treasurer of the artillery of the guard, secretly distributed wine and money to the soldiers in

Catherine's name, the Czar was busy at Oranienbaum making preparations to send an expedition against Denmark, determined to win back Schleswig, his hereditary province which he considered had been unjustly stolen from him. He was not only the Czar of Russia, but perhaps more important in his thinking, the Duke of Holstein. Had he been less of this mind and listened more to his spies and informants, his wife would doubtless have found it more difficult to plot against him.

'Are you sure you will not come with us? There is still time for you to go and change,' Anne said to Emma who stood beside her in the courtyard. Nikolai helped Lady Tarrant and her husband into the waiting carriage and then turned to her with a smile.

'I think perhaps our little cousin has other plans for tonight, my love. Boris Irienko was following her about last night at Sophie's house like a lovesick puppy. Did you take pity on him, Emma, and promise to have dinner with him this evening? He swore to me he would not leave you alone until you did.'

'No, I did not,' Emma laughed softly. 'I told him to go away and behave himself. I think he consoled his hurt feelings by going off with Maritza's friend, Natalie.'

'Then why are you staying at home?' Anne asked.

'Maritza does not feel too well. I think she drank just a little too much champagne yesterday. Believe me, I need the rest. Go and enjoy yourselves.'

How quiet the house was. Emma walked slowly back into the drawing-room, with the sound of the horses' hooves dying away in the distance. She rang for a maid and ordered a tray of food to be taken upstairs to Maritza at supper time and a samovar of coffee to be served directly for herself. She would spend a quiet evening reading, she decided.

As she approached the library, the sound of loud, angry voices slowed her steps. She heard Michael's voice in harsh tones.

'You fool, Passek! Did you have to throw yourself at

her feet like some comic actor. Didn't you realise we were being watched, man?'

The door was flung open as Emma hesitated. A uniformed figure, muttering under his breath, strode out. They had no chance to avoid each other, and Emma was sent staggering backwards against the wall, almost losing her balance.

'Damn your roughness, Passek. You will apologise to Mademoiselle Fraser at once.' An angry Michael appeared in the doorway.

Red faced, the young officer snapped to attention.

'Forgive me, mademoiselle, I was not looking where I was going. I trust you are not hurt?'

'Not at all,' Emma assured him.

Michael stared after his departing figure with a frown. He looked worried, she thought.

'I think I had better go after that young hot-head,' he said at length, 'before he does something else to attract attention.'

'Has he—been indiscreet?' Emma ventured to ask.

'Passek is a fool. No doubt you heard me tell him so. At a time when it is important for us to keep a firm grip on the unstable situation, that idiot created the biggest stir in St Petersburg since Catherine took her first lover. He threw himself at her feet, threatening to kill the Czar, before a room full of people. He will have us all in the fortress before long if someone doesn't still his tongue.'

Emma felt a cold hand clutch at her heart. She had never heard him speak this way before. Even though she knew where his loyalties lay, he had never openly declared them, and his manner, his choice of words, seemed to indicate he was not only totally involved in the plot to put Catherine on the throne, but was one of the leaders . . .

She was on her way back to the drawing-room when he came downstairs again. He had changed into a dark leather coat and hide breeches. Her eyes were drawn to the sword which hung at his side . . . only on very rare occasions had she seen him wear one before.

'Is there—nothing I can do to help? I know you are worried—and not only over this man Passek. For days you have been so preoccupied, even Nikolai has noticed it.'

Michael regarded her for a long moment, and then slowly nodded.

'Will you wait until I come back? I need to talk to someone. I may be late . . .'

'Yes,' Emma answered quietly. 'I will wait.'

'By the way, I took the liberty of having Madame Thérèse make a gown to replace the one which was ruined that night we went to Mon Plaisir. It was delivered this afternoon while you were out. I had it taken to your room. I hope you will find it suitable.'

'I am sure I will,' Emma said. 'It was very kind of you. I will look at it immediately.' She had seen the box in her sitting-room, but Maritza had called her away before she could investigate its contents, and she had forgotten it after that. Another yellow silk? she wondered, as she went upstairs.

Her fingers trembled as she lifted the lid and carefully pushed away the mass of wrapping paper enveloping the contents. Then she froze in disbelief, bewilderment, incredulity. It could not be . . . there had to be a mistake. Her hands were shaking still more as she lifted from the box a white satin and muslin wedding dress, complete with head-dress and train. It had been sent in error and she would return it first thing in the morning, she thought—but she could not resist the temptation to hold it against herself and look at her image in the mirror. It was breathtakingly beautiful, the full skirt slashed with lace insets, exactly as she had once sketched them for the wedding dress she dreamed of making for herself! The design was hers . . . there was no doubt about it. It was accurate in every detail. But how could Madame Thérèse have laid hands on her designs? Maritza was the only person who had ever seen them and that was only fleetingly, one afternoon. No! She was not the only one. Michael had come in and he had taken them to show Catherine. When he had returned them without a word, Emma had been disappointed she was not to make something new for the Czarina and had pushed them into a drawer without looking through them. Had she done so she would have realised one was missing.

In a daze she returned the dress to the box and then caught sight of the tiny white card which had fallen to the floor. It was in Michael's bold writing. 'The answer to my prayers lies in your acceptance of this,' he had written.

His prayers! He cared for her . . . more than that, if she understood his gift correctly . . . he loved her! It was not possible. He had said nothing, never indicated he harboured any deep feeling for her! Yet what else could the dress mean, but a proposal of marriage? Her heart was beating fiercely. She slid, weak-kneed, into a nearby chair. Was this why he wanted to talk to her upon his return? Was he expecting an answer?

There was only one, of course. The answer not only to his prayers, but to the most secret of her dreams . . . she was loved by a Prince! She could not keep such wonderful news to herself—she had to tell Maritza . . .

She opened the door of the girl's room very quietly so that she would not disturb her if she had fallen asleep—so quietly, in fact, she was able to take several paces into the room before she saw the cloaked figure hastily pushing clothes into the open valise on the bed.

'What are you doing?' Emma demanded. The headache had been an excuse.

Defiance flashed into Maritza's eyes as Emma advanced towards her. She snapped shut the bag and drew her cloak firmly around her.

'I thought you had gone out,' was all she said.

'You hoped I had, you mean. With everyone out of the house it would be easy for you to slip out unseen, leaving everyone to wonder where you had gone. Maritza—how could you even think of running away?'

'Vasily and I are going to be married,' Maritza declared and thrust her hand out for Emma to see the ring she wore. 'The Czar has given his permission for us to marry. Even Michael can't argue with him.'

'Maritza, you don't know what you are doing. Listen to me . . .' Emma pleaded. She could not allow the girl to leave the house, to go to a man whose suspicious behaviour over the past months had indicated that his allegiance was not to Catherine at all, but to Peter . . . a man who was ruthless enough to try and have murdered the brother of the girl he professed to love! 'Yes, you will listen. It is time you knew a little more of the man you intend to spend the rest of your life with. He is not the kind, adoring Vasily you think you know. He has lied and tricked you, probably from the first day you met him. It was he who sent an assassin after Michael the night of the ball at Mon Plaisir. I saw the two of them together, watched the blood-money change hands . . . money to murder your own brother! The coach was not attacked by a serf with a grudge against Michael. You were told that to spare your feelings. Even knowing what this man tried to do to him, he thought first of you . . .'

'No, no—you are lying. You and Michael would do anything to stop me marrying Vasily. But it's too late . . .' Picking up the bag she started towards the door. Emma sidestepped to try and prevent her reaching it, seized with the idea of locking her in her room until either Michael or Nikolai returned, but Maritza was too quick for her. A savage push sent her reeling back and by the time she had recovered her balance, the girl was running towards the stairs.

'Maritza—stop!'

She was half-way down the stairs when Maritza reached the door, only to come to a sudden halt as it opened without warning and Nikolai came in with Anne close on his heels. Emma could have wept with relief.

'Stop her,' she begged. 'She is going to Vasily Zouroff . . .'

'The devil she is!' A third figure stepped through the door, firmly closed it and stood with his back against it.

Emma's eyes widened in amazement as she stared at the uniform Michael wore . . . he looked exactly as he did in the portrait which hung over the fireplace. She heard Maritza whisper:

'Michael . . . why are you dressed like that? You resigned your commission years ago.' She looked from one brother to the other and then back at Emma, slowly moving to her side, and a look of terrible fear crossed her face. 'What is happening—someone tell me, please.'

'Michael never left the army, little one.' Nikolai's voice was gentle, as if to prepare her for what she was about to be told. 'Since the death of our father three years ago, he has been an active member of Catherine's secret service.'

For Emma his words made so many incidents fall into place. His close friendship with the Orloff brothers, especially Alexei who controlled the army's finances, and Gregory, Catherine's latest lover. Emma had never been able to understand why the two were such friends when they both sought the attentions of the same woman.

'Come with me, Maritza,' Anne said, slipping an arm around the girl's shoulders. 'It's time you and I had a talk. No, Nikolai, leave this to me,' she added as her husband stepped forward. 'You and Michael have things to do.'

Emma stood to one side as the two women passed her. She could see Maritza was on the point of breaking loose and trying to run, but Anne's grasp tightened around her, and she was led firmly upstairs. She turned and looked questioningly at the silent men standing by the door, noticing for the first time how pale and drawn they both looked. How did they come to be together? Nikolai had gone to the theatre, and Michael had raced after the young officer, Passek.

Michael strode past her into his study. A moment later he reappeared, grimly nodding his head.

'Jan was right—my desk has been rifled. Passek's arrest was unfortunate, but it changes nothing.'

'Arrest?' Emma echoed.

'At this very moment he is probably undergoing torture in the fortress, where Nikolai and I would have been later tonight, if Jan hadn't seen Zouroff climbing through the study window. Jan watched him and then followed when he left. He heard him give instructions for Passek's arrest. I am not the only one to have been playing a double-game, Emma. When Peter had rid himself of an unwanted wife and purged the army of loyal soldiers, Zouroff was to be rewarded for his services with the Adashev estates—and Maritza.' His mouth tightened into a bleak line as there came the sound of sobbing from upstairs. 'Anne has broken the news to her. Zouroff will betray no-one else. He is dead—Jan killed him as he was on his way to make a report to Peter. He saved me the task.'

Emma swallowed the natural horror which rose inside her. Vasily Zouroff would not have thought twice about disposing of his unwanted enemies had the position been reversed. She should save her pity for poor Maritza who would dearly need it in the days to come.

She had grown pale as she listened to Michael, shocked by the speedy turn of events which had almost, might still, take him from her, if the tide turned in Peter's favour tonight. She was apprehensive of the man who had so successfully led a double life for three years. And then, impulsively he strode across and caught her up in his arms, and his lips on hers proclaimed he was no stranger, but the man she loved.

She remained still in his embrace, his kisses lifting her to heights she had never before experienced, and the room swam about her as she clung to him, no longer able to deny herself the pleasure of his touch, the possessive pressure of his mouth on hers.

'You have the dress . . . you understood?' he murmured.

'Yes . . . yes. Oh, Michael, please let me go. I cannot think clearly like this,' she pleaded.

'Why should you? Tell me how you feel. Let me hear

you say it just once before I return to sanity.'

'I love you.'

He drew back, but still held tightly to her hands, pressing them against his breast. Beneath her fingers she could feel the fierce thudding of his heart. They were as one, she thought, as she desperately tried to gather her senses.

'Michael, you must go,' Nikolai said quietly.

'Yes. I rely on you to take care of the women, especially this impulsive English miss of mine.'

'Nikolai has known all along what you were doing?' Emma managed to stammer at last.

'For the last year,' Nikolai returned with a smile. 'He swore me to secrecy, and with so much at stake, I dared not confide in you, Emma, even when I realised you were falling in love with him.'

'Anne?'

'I had to tell her when Michael suddenly dragged me away from the theatre. She pretended to be unwell and we left the Tarrants there.'

'Poor Maritza,' Emma said, looking towards the stairs. 'Do you think she will ever trust anyone again?'

'Time heals all wounds.' Michael pressed her fingers to his lips. 'I must ride like the wind if I am to catch the others. Tell her, Nikolai,' he commanded, as Emma opened her mouth to question him, and then he was gone.

'Where—where is he going?' Her voice shook. What if he were hurt? Or killed in a fight with the Czar's soldiers? Catherine was about to seize the throne of Russia—there would be fighting and killing . . .

'The Orloff's are taking the Czarina to Kalinkina, a village some miles from here where the Ismailovsky regiment has its headquarters. We have to rally the soldiers—persuade them she is in imminent danger from the Czar. Michael rides ahead to organise his men in the Preobrazhensky . . .'

'His friendship with the Czarina made it possible for him to come and go at court. Together with the Orloffs he has been planning this day for many months.'

'Catherine is not—not his . . .' Emma could not bring herself to finish, as a smile came to Nikolai's face.

'Hasn't he made it quite clear there is only one woman in his life—you? Ever since he came back from France and told me about you, he has been like a man possessed. His dangerous situation made him hesitate to approach you openly. He could not tell you what he was involved in, and when you made it plain you thought he was having an affair with Catherine, he dared not speak. I told him he was a fool. He loved you . . . he should have asked for your trust.'

'Nikolai, wait . . . what has France to do with it? I know it was there he first saw Anne . . .'

'Haven't you realised, he also chose a wife for himself? Included in the terms of the agreement the Tarrants accepted, was the condition you accompany Anne to Russia. He wanted you—loved you from the first time he saw you in that yellow dress. I felt sure he had given himself away when you wore one of the same colour to the wedding and Maritza told me he had chosen it for you . . .'

Emma straightened her cramped limbs, straining her ears for the sound of hoofbeats on the cobbles outside, but only the lonely hooting of an owl in the trees behind the house broke the silence of her long vigil. She had been curled up on the window seat in the drawing-room for the past three hours, ever since Nikolai had at last accepted that she would not go to bed until Michael had returned safe and sound.

They had spent an hour trying to calm Maritza's hysterics and in the end it had been Anne who had taken the girl in her arms and rocked her to sleep like a little baby. The pride in Nikolai's eyes as he watched his wife helped to ease a little of Emma's own distress.

He had greeted the Tarrants upon their return to the house with such smiles and easy conversation that Emma began to wonder if the whole unpleasant evening had been no more than a dream. He was as adept at concealing his true feelings as was his brother. On this occasion, she was more than grateful.

France—it had all begun in France! And at the inn Michael had come to inspect the prospective bride—to be sure of the choice he had made, but which one of them had really brought him chasing across the country-side in such abominable weather? She wondered if she would ever have the courage to ask him.

It was almost dawn before a horse turned into the courtyard. She watched him climb down slowly—so slowly in fact that for one awful minute she thought he had been injured. Then he straightened and came into the house. She met him at the door, trembling, bright tears brimming in her eyes as they scanned his face, his body, for some sign of what he might have been through.

In silence he lifted her and carried her into the drawing-room, his lips lightly brushing her hair, her face, finally her mouth as he sank down with her onto the couch.

Emma raised her head.

'Was that Jan with you?'

'Yes, thanks to him we were able to act before Passek talked. I was able to warn others they were in danger. We suffered few casualties.' He relaxed back onto the cushions with a tired sigh. His fingers gently stroked Emma's hair as she rested her cheek against his shoulder, content to remain within the circle of his arms.

'You should have seen them, Emma—the soldiers rose to her side *en masse*. People came out to follow her carriage all the way back to the city.'

'And—and the Czar?'

'A few hours from now he will be on his way to Mon Plaisir. He will not find Catherine waiting for him, however. At this very moment she is in the Kazan Cathedral, being blessed by the bishop before a crowd of hundreds.'

'Surely you should be there,' she murmured. This was his moment too. Had he not risked his life to see it happen? Yet he wanted none of the glory which came with it, shunned the opportunity to stand at the side of the new Empress of Russia.

'What I wanted was here—not in the Kazan,' he whispered, his mouth against hers.

The servant opened the door and then went away without a word. Michael glanced up as it closed again.

'This is the second time I have compromised you, Emma Fraser, do you realise that? We have set the servants talking again. We must marry soon. I have found these past months unbearable.'

'Yes, monseigneur,' Emma murmured meekly.

'Don't say that. I am not your master.'

She raised her face to his, her eyes shining.

'I shall love and serve you faithfully for the rest of my life. You are my master—my own true love—forever!'